Slocum topped a rise on the little roan, and he saw a gathering of men down below him and a distance ahead. He found a place where he could dismount, hide the horse, and settle himself down snug behind a large boulder. He took a pair of binoculars out of his saddlebag and studied the gang down below and ahead. Right away, he recognized Ace Carter. He looked carefully at each man, studied each face. He wanted to be sure he would never forget any one of those seven men. He meant to kill them all for what they had done to Harley.

He put away the spy glasses and took out his Winchester. Cranking a shell into the chamber, he settled down again against the big rock. He made himself comfortable and took careful aim, but it was a long shot. Perhaps, he thought, a shot down among them would scare them all back to Whizbang. That was where he really wanted them. In Whizbang they would separate. They would go to their individual homes and individual jobs. He could wait a while, let them relax, then slip up on them one at a time.

He sighted in on Carter and squeezed the trigger . . .

JAKE LOGAN

SLOCUM'S PARTNER

JOVE BOOKS, NEW YORK

This is a work of fiction. Names, characters, places, and incidents are
either the product of the author's imagination or are used fictitiously,
and any resemblance to actual persons, living or dead, business
establishments, events, or locales is entirely coincidental.

SLOCUM'S PARTNER

A Jove Book / published by arrangement with
the author

PRINTING HISTORY
Jove edition / August 2000

All rights reserved.
Copyright © 2000 by Penguin Putnam Inc.
This book may not be reproduced in whole or in part,
by mimeograph or any other means, without permission.
For information address: The Berkley Publishing Group,
a division of Penguin Putnam Inc.,
375 Hudson Street, New York, New York 10014.

The Penguin Putnam Inc. World Wide Web site address is
http://www.penguinputnam.com

ISBN: 0-515-12889-9

A JOVE BOOK®
Jove Books are published by The Berkley Publishing Group,
a division of Penguin Putnam Inc.,
375 Hudson Street, New York, New York 10014.
JOVE and the "J" design
are trademarks belonging to Penguin Putnam Inc.

PRINTED IN THE UNITED STATES OF AMERICA

10 9 8 7 6 5 4 3 2 1

1

Slocum had been having himself a grand old time all night long with the lovely and frisky Darlene, a long-legged blonde, and just in the next room, his new and best friend, Harley Duggan, was having just as good a time with Darlene's dark and sultry friend, Simone. All night long, Darlene had done everything with Slocum that he knew about or could imagine, and then she had gone on and done even more. A hell of a night, he thought. He couldn't have asked for more, but he could see daylight coming in through the window, and he was hungry as hell. With his right hand, he reached over casually and slapped Darlene on her round bare ass. It made a loud smacking sound, and she yelped like a pup whose tail had been stepped on, and sat up quick and straight, snapping her head around and giving him a hard look.

"What the hell was that for?" she asked, setting her full lips in a hard pout.

"Let's go on out and have us some breakfast," he said.

"Well, don't you think we had ought to get ourselves dressed first?" she asked him.

"That's likely a good idea," he agreed.

"The only reason I asked you that," she said, "is 'cause you never said nothing about us getting dressed first. You just only said let's go out and get breakfast, so I thought

I'd better ask. For all I know you wanted to go walking nekkid through the streets. You never said—"

"Come on," Slocum said, interrupting her and ignoring her sarcasm. It was a quality of hers that he did not admire. "Get dressed." He had already pulled on his jeans and was reaching for his boots. He picked up the boots and sat back on the edge of the bed to pull them on. Darlene suddenly romped across the bed like a frenzied wildcat and grabbed him tightly around the shoulders. She pulled him down on the bed backwards and leaned over his face, pressing her open and moist lips hard against his mouth. He humored her, and they had a long, deep, wet kiss. At last, gasping for breath, she backed off. "Get dressed," he said.

By the time Slocum had pulled his shirt on, Darlene was just about half dressed. "Do you think we should call Simone and Harley to go out and eat with us?" she asked. Slocum looked at the wall between the two rooms. He waited a few seconds before answering her question, and in their silence they could hear happy moans and giggles, even the squeaking of bed springs, coming through the wall from the next room. Harley and Simone were obviously still very much involved. He looked back at Darlene. "What do you think?" he said.

She said, "I guess not."

He fastened his shirt and tucked the tail in his trousers. Then he strapped on his gunbelt with his Colt. He picked up his hat and looked at Darlene again. She still wasn't ready. "It sure takes a mess of clothes to cover up your pretty body," he said. Just then there was a crashing sound, as if a door had been kicked in. It was followed by a scream and shouts. Darlene jumped and squealed.

"What's that?" she asked. Slocum didn't answer. He just slapped the hat on his head and ran out the door. Turning sharply, he saw that the door to the next room was standing wide open. He moved cautiously into the doorway, and found himself standing behind the back of a big stranger. The man was leveling a revolver at the two naked figures huddled together in the bed.

"No, Carl," Simone said, her voice a desperate whimper.

"I'll kill you both," Carl said. "Damn you." He thumbed back the hammer, and Slocum pulled his Colt fast, raised it high over his head, and brought it down hard on Carl's head. Carl stiffened first, then relaxed and fell forward like a dropped flour sack. Slocum put away his Colt and picked up Carl's revolver.

"Just in time, partner," Harley said. "That son of a bitch was fixing to shoot me in all my nekkid glory."

"Not just you," Simone protested.

"Let's get the hell out of here," said Slocum.

Harley turned to Simone. "Will you be all right?" he asked her. "You want to come along with us?"

"No," she said. "I'll be all right."

"Who is that son of a bitch anyway?" Harley asked her.

"He's my husband," she said. "Just go. Go on now. Hurry, before he wakes up."

"Your husband?" Harley said. "You never said—"

"I didn't think he'd be back till tomorrow night," Simone said. "You'd better go on and get out now. I mean it."

"You sure you'll be all right?" Harley asked. "He said he was going to kill you."

"Don't worry," she said. "I can handle him. He's said that before."

"Hurry it up," Slocum said. "Listen to the lady."

Darlene pushed her way past Slocum just then to run over and crawl in bed beside Simone. She put an arm around Simone's shoulder and hugged her tight. "Oh, honey," she said. "It's all right now. Don't worry. I'll stay right here with you."

Slocum picked up Harley's shirt and hat and threw them across the room at Harley. "Get them on," he said. "I'll go get the horses and meet you out back."

"Okay, pard," Harley said.

Slocum hurried down to the stable where he and Harley had boarded their horses the day before, and in a few minutes he had them both saddled and ready to ride. Mounting his big Appaloosa, he led Harley's roan down the alley behind the hotel. Harley soon came out on the landing and rushed down the stairs to join him. They rode fast out of town headed west. A few miles safely down the road, Slocum and Harley Duggan slowed their mounts and from there they rode along at a leisurely pace.

"So, he was her husband, huh?" Slocum said. "Since when did you start taking up with other men's wives? I never did cotton to stealing another man's wife. Is that a habit with you? I didn't know you was like that, Harley."

"I never knew she had no husband, but that's what she said right after you knocked him cold," Harley answered. "And he surely did act thataway, didn't he? I mean, you know, like he was mighty offended. I reckon she really is his damned wife, but hell, Slocum, I never knew. Besides, I never meant to steal her, just to borry her for a while."

"You reckon you ought to be more careful 'bout how you pick your women from here on out?" Slocum asked.

"Why, you old son of a bitch," Harley said, "I never really even picked her. I never. You know that. You done it, damn it. It was you. Leastways, you done had that Darlene already picked out for yourself, and it was her that brung her friend Simone along. You remember that, don't you?"

"Yeah," said Slocum, "I recall, but you don't need to just take everything that's handed to you without asking no questions. It ain't my fault that you wound up in bed with a married woman. It's my fault that you're still alive though. That's my fault for sure. I got to live with that on my conscience now."

"I reckon you do at that, partner," Harley said. "And you can bet I won't never forget it neither."

Slocum enjoyed the company of Harley Duggan, and he enjoyed the good-natured banter. He had spent years traveling alone, and it was good to have a companion for a change. He had thought that he preferred going through life with only his own company, but he reckoned now that he just hadn't run across the right person to partner with. He recalled how he had met Harley back in Sloan's Corner. Slocum had been the big winner in a poker game and the other players had accused him of cheating. Before he knew what was happening, he found himself fighting off three men. He was holding his own pretty well until a fourth had come up behind him and raised up a chair with the full intention of bashing his brains out with it. That was when Harley had appeared on the scene.

Harley had jerked the chair out of the man's hands and then downed him with one powerful punch. Then, having put himself into the fight already, he stepped up beside Slocum to help deal with the original three. Together, it hadn't taken Slocum and Harley long to finish off those three. Soon there were four toughs lying on the floor out cold, and Slocum had his winnings in his pockets. Slocum asked Harley how he had come to get in the fight, and all Harley had said was, "I didn't like the odds."

They had a couple of drinks together after that, and it seemed to Slocum as if he had known Harley Duggan for years, even though he well knew he had never set eyes on the man before the fight. Then they had decided that the four on the floor might wake up and have ideas about getting even. They might try sneaking up behind them, or they might have some friends they could get together. Then they had ridden out of Sloan's Corner together.

By the time Slocum and Harley had stopped over in Lone Grove and hooked up with Darlene and Simone, they had been riding together for several weeks. Slocum was real comfortable with Harley riding along by his side. "Where do we go from here, partner?" Harley asked, interrupting Slocum's musings.

"Hell," said Slocum, "I don't know. We still got money in our jeans. Don't need to work. I figure we'll just ride along and take it easy and see what we might run up against."

"Take it as it comes, huh?" said Harley. "Hell, that suits me just fine."

They continued along their leisurely way until the sun was high in the sky and their bellies were beginning to complain of neglect. They watched for a likely camping spot, and when they came to a small bubbling brook, they stopped and unsaddled their horses. While the horses drank and grazed, Harley built a small fire, and Slocum dug out what they had between them to use for a meal: a tin of beans, some hardtack, and some jerky. They also had coffee, and he set some on to boil. Life was pretty good.

"Next town we come to," Slocum said, "I sure don't want you chasing after no women right off. You and your women always get you into trouble, and when you get into trouble, I have to come and get you out of it. So you just put yourself on your best behavior for a while."

"Seems like just the opposite was the way we met, partner," Harley said. "Seems like it was me had to come and get you out of trouble."

"Well, that was then," said Slocum. "This is now. You just take it easy with the women. That's all. Besides, I could have handled all four of them bastards by myself."

It was all good-natured teasing, and both men understood it and took part in it in that spirit. They ate their fill and drank plenty of coffee. Then Slocum lit a cigar and leaned back to enjoy a good smoke. "If you want yourself a bath," he said, "go on in now. I'll keep a watch till you're done. Then you can watch, and I'll go get wet."

"Sounds good to me," Harley said. "Even though I had me a bath just last month."

Harley was in the water when the riders approached the small camp. There were four of them. Slocum saw them coming and stood up to meet them. They stopped a few feet short of the camp and sat on their horses, looking at Slocum. He was looking them over too and he didn't like what he saw. A rough-looking bunch, they had the smell of hide hunters about them. They had the weapons for it too. One of the four nudged his horse a little forward of the other three. "Howdy," he said.

Slocum nodded. "Howdy."

"You camping here alone, are you?" the man said.

"Looks that way," Slocum said, "don't it?"

"You got two horses over there," the man said.

"You got good eyes," said Slocum.

Harley kept himself in the water up to his chin, and he

was down behind some tall grass that grew along the bank. His clothes and his sidearm were close by in the grass. He watched and listened.

"Might be we'd be interested in buying a horse," the big dirty man said.

"I'm fond of both them horses," said Slocum. "They ain't for sale."

"You got a fire going," said the hide hunter. "You been cooking a meal for yourself?"

"I did," Slocum said.

"You got enough for four hungry travelers?"

"I ate up everything I had," Slocum said. "Even drank the last of my coffee. Got nothing to offer you."

"I don't believe him, Ned," said one of the other hunters.

"Joseph don't believe you," said Ned. "Could it be that you got more food and coffee and cigars, and you just don't want to share it none with weary traveling men?"

"Think what you want," Slocum said.

"You know," said Ned, "there's a code out here, a kind of unwrote law, that says when you got a home or a camp and weary travelers come by, you invite them in and share what you got with them. You might be in need yourself some day."

"I take care of myself pretty good," Slocum said.

"Let's see how good he takes care of hisself, Ned," said Joseph.

Slocum steadied himself for a quick draw, and said, "Why don't you men just ride on out of here and live a while longer?"

One of the hitherto silent men said, "You pig shit," and jerked out a pistol, raising it at arm's length to point at Slocum, but just as it was about level, a shot rang out and blood splattered out the side of his face. The other three reached for their guns. Slocum's Colt was out fast. His first shot slammed into Ned's chest. Ned's face took on a silly look as he tilted his head forward to examine the hole down there. Blood seeped out onto his dirty shirt, and he reeled in the saddle. A second shot from the brook's edge ripped into the rib cage of Joseph, as Slocum's second shot dropped the fourth man from the back of his horse. He hit the ground and bounced, raising a cloud of dust.

Keeping his Colt ready for action, Slocum walked toward the four men, now all lying on the ground and bleeding. He stopped first beside Ned. The big man was lying on his back, breathing hard and looking up at Slocum. Slocum kicked Ned's gun away. "It was a dirty trick," said Ned. "They's two of you, by God." Slocum walked over to check the other three. Two of them were dead. The one that Harley had shot in the side of the face was still wriggling some. Slocum picked up the wounded man's gun. Just then Harley, stark naked and dripping wet, walked up. He stopped by Ned and looked down on him. Drops of water fell from Harley's body and splattered on Ned's face. Ned blinked.

"Kilt by a nekkid man," he said, and then he died.

"Anyone else still alive?" Harley asked Slocum.

"The first one you shot," Slocum said. "Over there."

Harley walked gingerly on his bare feet over to look at the man. He made a face. "He's a goddamn mess," he said. "He can't live much longer like that, can he? Shot right through the face?"

"I seen them live with their jaws shot clean off," Slocum said. "They ain't never pretty afterwards though."

"Yeah," Harley said, "but that's if a doc gets hold of them, too. Out here like this, hell, he'll just bleed to death. That's all. I wouldn't wish that kind of slow dying on no one, not a damn mangy dog."

Without another word or any other kind of warning, Harley pointed his revolver and fired point-blank into the man's chest, killing him instantly. Startled, Slocum jumped and turned around. He gave Harley a questioning look.

"Well, damn it, would you want to just lay around suffering and bleeding and whimpering like that?" Harley said. "Way out here in the middle of nowhere? I know I wouldn't. I sure as hell wouldn't. Hell, I just done him a favor is all."

"Get dressed," Slocum said, and his face was grim. "You look silly like that."

"Hey, ol' partner," Harley said. "We still work pretty damn good together, don't we?"

Harley dressed himself while Slocum started digging graves some distance away from their camp. Soon Harley joined him in dragging the bodies of the nasty hide hunters over and dumping them unceremoniously into the holes. Then they covered them over and walked back to their camp. They unsaddled the hide hunters' horses.

"We going to turn them loose?" Harley asked.

"We could," Slocum said. "It ain't the most friendly surroundings I've ever seen for horses though. Especially for tame horses."

"We could take them with us," Harley said. "Sell them maybe."

"Yeah," said Slocum. "Maybe."

2

Three days later, they rode into the small town of Whiz-bang leading four extra saddle horses. As Slocum had told Harley, they really didn't need the money, but it seemed a shame to just leave the horses behind. After all, their owners were dead out in the middle of nowhere. Slocum suggested that they contact the law in Whizbang and tell the tale of how they came to have the horses and then let the law decide what should be done with the animals. Might be they'd be allowed to sell them. They rode into town late in the day, and the town marshal's office was locked up. Then they stopped in front of the local saloon, called the Booze Palace, tied all six horses to the hitch rail outside, and went in for some long overdue refreshment.

At the bar Slocum ordered a bottle of whiskey and two glasses. When the bartender put them in front of him, he paid the man, and then asked, "Where might I find the town marshal?"

"You won't find him in town," the bartender said. "Not till day after tomorrow. He's off on some kind of lawman business."

"Is there a deputy?" Slocum asked.

The barkeep shook his head. "We got a pretty small town here. We can barely pay the marshal's keep. Don't think it's a wide-open town, though. There's plenty of folks around who watches over things while the law's away. We got a lot of pride in our little community here. You might say we're civic-minded folks."

"Thanks," Slocum said. He picked up the bottle and a glass. Harley took the other glass, and the partners found themselves an empty table. They sat down across from one another, and Slocum poured them each a drink. A couple of tables down, a big man in a three-piece suit sitting with three other men stood up. Carrying his glass, he walked over to where Slocum and Harley sat, hooked his thumbs in the sleeve holes of his vest, and looked down at them.

"You're strangers in town," he said.

"That's obvious to everyone here," said Slocum.

"You got names?" said the big man.

"Most folks do," said Harley. "What about you? You got one?"

"All right," the man said. "I reckon I set myself up for that one. I'm Ace Carter. I own this place. Mind if I sit down?"

Harley gestured toward an empty chair. "Like you said," he answered, "it's your place."

Carter pulled out the chair and sat. "Thanks," he said. "I don't mean to seem nosy, but our town marshal is out of town for a spell, and we're real community-minded folks here in Whizbang."

"So we've heard," Slocum said. "Okay. My name's John Slocum. My partner here is Harley Duggan. We're just traveling. Passing through here, you might say. It's been a long, dusty trail. Some good whiskey, a few good meals, and a little rest will help us move on down the road. Is there anything else you'd like to know?"

"No, I guess not," Carter said with a shrug. "You got a place to stay?"

"Not yet," Slocum said.

"There's a nice rooming house two doors down," Carter said. "Reasonable rates. Clean rooms. It's called Trumbull's. Chilly Trumbull's a friend of mine. A good solid citizen. Runs a good establishment. Right on the other side of him is Millicent's Eatery. You won't find better food anywhere around for miles. Enjoy your stay, boys. If you don't cause any trouble, we'll treat you right."

Carter stood up and walked back to his own table to rejoin his companions there. They all gave the strangers the eye. Slocum and Harley looked at one another. "Harley," said Slocum, "you recall that little grove of cottonwoods just outside of town? Little creek running past?"

"Yeah," Harley said. "Pretty little spot."

"What do you say we make our camp out there?" Slocum said.

"You mean, away from all these upstanding civic-minded folks?" Harley said.

"Yeah," said Slocum. "Something like that."

They drained their glasses. Slocum picked up the bottle, and they walked out of the Booze Palace. "We might try that eating place, though," Harley said, "before we go on out yonder. I'm getting kind of tired of eating your beans." Slocum agreed, and they walked down the street to Millicent's Eatery. Millicent's had only a few customers, and most of them were finishing up. Slocum and Harley found themselves a table that was almost clean and sat down at it. Shortly, a youngish woman in a dress and a greasy apron came over to the table. She was obviously tired from a long day's work, but she smiled pleasantly at them.

"Hi there," she said. "I'm Millicent. Welcome. What can I get for you?"

"Well now," said Harley, giving Millicent a good looking over, "we just came in here to eat, but right now I'm wondering what you might be doing later on."

Slocum gave Harley's shin a kick under the table, and Harley yowled. "Don't pay any attention to my partner here, ma'am," Slocum said. "He ain't housebroke yet. We'd like some coffee and your best steak dinners."

Millicent gave Slocum a friendly smile. Then she glanced at Harley. "That's all right," she said. "I'll bring your coffee right over and get your dinners started." As she walked away, Slocum couldn't help but notice the gentle swing of her hips. She was a fine-looking woman, and he really couldn't blame Harley a bit for making a try at her, however clumsy. Harley leaned over to rub his shin. His face winced with pain.

"What the hell'd you do that for?" he said.

"You was fixing to get us into trouble again," Slocum said. "That was just a gentle reminder. That's all."

"Damn it," Harley said. "That hurt."

Millicent came back with the coffee. Harley gave her a sheepish smile, and Slocum thanked her kindly. She swung away again, and both men watched. They couldn't help themselves. "She looks just fine," Harley said. "She'd be worth a little trouble."

"Drink your coffee," said Slocum. "I don't want to have to rescue you again." Harley picked up his cup and took a sip.

"She'd be worth a lot of trouble," he said. "Hell, you don't want to come to my rescue, you don't have to. I'll take care of myself."

"Harley, you remember all those fine upstanding citizens we just met?" Slocum asked. "And no law in town? You mind your manners, damn it."

Millicent brought their meals over, and they tied into them like they hadn't eaten in a week. They drank more coffee, and when they were finally finished, Slocum said, "I want you to take all them horses out there but mine and ride on out yonder to set up our camp."

"And just what the hell are you going to be doing?" Harley asked.

"Not that it's any of your damn business," Slocum said, "but I'm going to get us some eggs and bacon for the morning and a bottle of whiskey for tonight. Then I'll be right along to keep you company."

Harley took another long and wistful look at Millicent, and Slocum said, "Get going. I'll pay for this, gather that stuff up and be along directly. Go on now. I want you the hell out of town. I mean it."

"Aw, hell," Harley said, but he scooted his chair back and stood up. He hesitated, but Slocum stared hard at him, and he slouched on out of Millicent's. There were only two other customers left in the place, and a moment or two after Harley left, they got up to pay for their meals and left. Slocum was alone in the room. He drained his coffee cup, and before he could even put it down on the table, Millicent was there with the coffeepot. She was holding a cup in her other hand.

"Refill?" she asked.

"Sure," Slocum said. "Thanks." Millicent poured his cup full.

"Mind if I join you?" she said.

"I sure don't mind," Slocum said, and Millicent sat down and poured herself a cup.

"It's been a long day," she said.

"I reckon it has been," said Slocum.

"Where's your friend?" she asked.

"Ol' Harley?" Slocum said. "My partner? I sent him on out of town to set up our camp. I figured I'd get him out of town to keep him out of trouble."

Millicent chuckled, and Slocum liked the sound of her voice. "Is he really so bad?" she asked.

"Last town we were in," Slocum said, "he got caught in bed with another man's wife. I slugged the man, and we high-tailed it out of town. I got to watch him all the time."

"Why do you keep him around?" she asked.

"He jumped right in the middle of a fight to help me out once," Slocum said. "That's how we met. And he ain't really bad company."

Millicent looked at Slocum as if considering something, as if she wanted to say something but hadn't quite made up her mind if it was such a good idea. At last she said, "You know, I've got my rooms just in back of the place here. I've also got something a little stronger than this black coffee to drink. Would you care to join me?"

"I surely would," Slocum said. He stood up, then moved around to pull her chair back for her.

"Let me lock up the front," she said.

Slocum watched her move across the room and congratulated himself on his good fortune. He tried to imagine what Harley would say when he found out about this. Why, ol' Harley might just punch him in the jaw.

Out in the street, Harley was sulking some at having been sent out of town by Slocum to get the camp ready. He was mounted up though, and about to lead the string of the extra four horses out to the campsite, but a devious thought entered his head. He turned and looked at Slocum's big Appaloosa. A man came walking down the street and gave Harley a look. He paused, then went into the Booze Palace. Harley paid him no mind, but instead grinned and said out loud to himself, "It'll serve ol' Slocum right." He rode over close to the Appaloosa, leaned over, and loosed the reins from the rail, then rode out of town, leading Slocum's horse along with the others. He started to laugh at his joke.

Inside the Booze Palace, Ace Carter still sat drinking with his companions when the man from outside walked over to his table, a look of concern on his face. "Howdy, Morley," Carter said. "Pull up a chair and join us."

The man called Morley sat down, and Carter offered him a drink. Morley accepted it, but continued with his stern expression. "What's eating at you?" Carter asked. Morley downed the drink in a gulp and shoved the glass toward Carter for a refill. Carter obliged.

"I just now saw a cowboy ride out of town leading four of Tom Grant's horses," Morley said.

"Are you sure about that?" Carter asked.

"Sure as any goddamn thing," said Morley. "I bought a horse from ol' Tom a while back. Looked over his whole string real good then, I did. I'd recognize them anywhere."

"What did this cowhand look like?" Carter asked. Morley shrugged.

"Like a cowhand," he said. "Young smooth-faced fellow. Wearing a big white hat. Red shirt, I think. Vest."

Carter looked from one to another of his drinking companions. "That was one of them two that was in here," said one of the men.

"Sure sounds like it," said another.

"Morley," said Carter, "was there another man with him?"

"Well," said Morley, "I only seen one."

"You see which way he rode out of town?" Carter asked.

"Sure, I did," Morley said.

"Come on," Carter said, and every man at the table stood to follow him out.

Slocum sat beside Millicent on a couch in her small quarters behind the cafe. She had poured two glasses of brandy and put them on a table there before the couch. "Is it Miss Millicent?" he asked her.

"It's Mrs. Millicent Walters," she said. "I lost my husband about a year ago in an accident."

"Sorry," Slocum said.

"That's all right," she said.

"How come you invited me back here tonight?" he asked.

"That's a fair question," she said. "It's not a habit of mine, if that's what you're getting at. You're the first man I've had back here. I thought about it pretty hard before I asked you. I guess I felt like it would be disloyal to him, but—"

"But he's gone," Slocum said, "and you're still a lovely lady. Still young."

"Thank you," she said.

"But why me?" he said.

She shrugged. "I don't know," she said. "You're a good-looking guy, but that's not all. There have been other good-looking guys come in my place. Some have made passes at me, and I turned them away. So it's not just that. I like you."

"You don't even know me," Slocum said.

"No," she agreed, "but I like you anyway. I like the way you took care of your friend. I like the way you talk. I don't know. Maybe it's just that tonight's the night, after a year of being lonely."

"Well," he said, "I'm glad I happened in here on this particular night. The only thing is, ol' Harley's going to be mad as hell if he ever finds out about this."

She laughed a soft laugh as he reached his arm around her to pull her close and kiss her soft lips. He could tell right away that she was eager. The closeness of her, her touch and smell, made him eager as well.

Harley had just built up a small fire when he heard the horses coming. He stepped back out of the light and checked the looseness of the revolver in the holster by his side. Then he saw Ace Carter riding with six other men. He relaxed a little, but he was curious. "Howdy," he said, "what can I do for you?"

Carter nodded toward the horses. "Is that them?" he asked.

"They's the ones," Morley said.

"Where'd you get those horses?" Carter asked Harley.

"One's mine," Harley said. "One's my partner's. The other four is part of the reason we come into town asking for the marshal. Four hide hunters set on us a few days ago, and we killed them. We decided to bring their horses along with us and ask the law what to do with them."

"A likely story," Carter said.

"You stole them horses from poor ol' Tom Grant," Morley said. "Like to have killed him too. Left him for dead, but he fooled you, all right. He's still hanging on."

"Whoa," said Harley. "Wait just a minute there. I don't know nothing about no horse stealing or no Tom Grant neither. We come by these horses just like I told you. Never been in these parts before."

"Where's your partner?" Carter asked.

"I left him in town," Harley said. "I come out ahead to set up camp."

"You left him in town without his horse?" said Carter.

"Well, it was, it was like a joke," said Harley. "You know?"

"Get his gun, boys," Carter said. Two shotguns were raised and pointed at Harley. Two men dismounted and moved to his side. One relieved him of his revolver while yet another slapped at his body checking for any other weapons he might have secreted away. No others were found. The two men stayed close by Harley.

"Well, all right," Harley said. "Take me on in. We'll get this mess all cleared up in the morning. I guess I don't mind spending a night in jail."

"Why wait till morning?" said Morley.

"What do you mean?" Harley asked.

"Where's your partner?" said Carter.

"I told you," Harley said. "I left him in town."

"I know how to make him talk," said one of the men. He rode over to a nearby tree while paying out his rope. Underneath a low hanging branch, he tossed the rope over. "Bring him on over here."

"Hey," Harley said. "Wait a minute. Take me on in to the jailhouse. You can check on my story tomorrow. You'll find out it's all true. Just like I said."

The two men standing near him grabbed his arms, and Harley started to struggle. Two more men dismounted and ran to join the struggle. Harley kicked and jerked, but eventually the men had his arms tied behind him, and they dragged him to where the noosed rope dangled from the tree branch. One slipped the noose around Harley's neck.

"Where's your partner?" Ace Carter asked.

"In town," said Harley.

"Lift him up a bit," Carter said, and the mounted man with the rope backed his horse until the rope tightened around Harley's throat. Harley grit his teeth and tightened his neck. He gagged and coughed as he felt himself being lifted off the ground by the tightening noose around his neck. He felt his face swelling, felt as if it would burst. "That's enough," Carter said. "Let him down." Harley felt his feet touch the ground again. The rope was still tight. He gasped for breath in between coughs and gagging. "Where's your partner?" said Carter.

Slocum's hand went around Millicent's soft throat, then slid up to the side of her face. He kissed her lips, and she let them part to allow his tongue to probe the inside of her mouth. He ran his hand down the side of her face, along her neck and shoulder and down to a soft but firm and round breast. He squeezed it gently, and she moaned. Then his hand crept down her side, down her leg, and found the hem of her dress. It reached under, then crept up the inside of her thigh to her warm, wet crotch.

"Wait," she said, and Slocum backed off. Millicent stood up and started to take off her clothes. Slocum sat and watched her as she revealed first her lovely breasts, then her legs, then finally her full nakedness. He stood facing her, and she started to undress him. By the time she finished, he was standing fully erect.

"He's a stubborn son of a bitch," Morley said.

"Let him down," Carter said.

The rider eased his horse forward until Harley's feet touched the ground, but the rope was still taut. He moved forward a bit more. The rope stayed stretched, and Harley's body slumped limp at its end. "Take him down," Carter ordered. "Hurry it up." And two men took hold of Harley's arms. Another loosened the noose and pulled it off Harley's head. They laid him out on the ground, and one bent over him. Then he looked up at Carter. His eyes were wide and his face was ashen.

"He's dead," the man said. "We killed the son of a bitch."

Slocum lay on top of Millicent, pounding his pelvis against hers. He felt himself drive over and over his full length into her warm wet channel of delight. At last he knew that it was over. He felt the surge, and he spurted again and again until he was spent. He lay still, and she held him tight in her arms.

It was later when he finally dressed and told her that he had to go. "If I don't show up at the camp pretty soon," he said, "ol' Harley's liable to come looking for me."

"I understand," she said, and she kissed him a fond farewell. "Will I see you again?" she asked.

"That's likely," he said. "It's been a real fine evening."

• • •

Stepping out into the street, he was thinking that Harley was going to be really pissed off at him for this. He was almost to the hitching rail in front of the saloon before he realized that his horse was nowhere in sight. Then he figured it out. The little shit, he said to himself. I'll kick his ass for this. It was a long walk out to the campsite, but there was nothing else to do. He set out. He had not quite reached the edge of town when he heard the sound of several horses coming fast toward him. He stepped into a shadow beside a building and waited. Then he saw the seven riders coming back into town. He saw Ace Carter in the lead. Then he saw the six extra horses, and even in the dark, he recognized them as the horses of the four dead hide hunters, Harley's, and his own.

He watched as the riders pulled up in front of the Booze Palace. No one bothered to stable the horses. They left them there as they went inside. Slocum cautiously made his way back to the saloon in shadows. Sidling up to the window in the front, he peered in to see Carter and the others pouring themselves drinks. He looked up and down the street, saw no one watching, hurried out to the side of his big Appaloosa and mounted up. Then he raced out of town and toward the campsite.

It seemed a much longer ride out than he remembered it, even though he was running his horse hard. At last he saw the flicker of the untended fire. A small one, it had not been fed for a spell. It would burn out soon. Slocum slowed his pace as he rode into the camp. Then he saw that it was really no camp at all. There was nothing but the neglected fire. There was no sign of life. He dismounted and started to look around.

The night was dark, but the sky was clear. The silence was heavy and ominous. The crunch of his own footsteps sounded to Slocum like major rude intrusions into the stillness. He heard no bird calls, no distant coyote howls, not even the humming of insects. As his ears strained at the quiet, the rippling of the nearby brook did finally reach him.

Near the fire he could see some footprints, but it was too dark to follow them out away from the fire. He would not be able to tell much until daylight. But where was Harley? He walked around, looking, knowing that he was destroying tracks as he did, but looking for Harley would not wait for daylight. He moved farther and farther away from the tiny fire in his search, and then, all at once, he saw the body. "Oh God," he said. He rushed to it, hoping to find some life still in it. He dropped to his knees and lifted the head. It was Harley all right, and Slocum could tell right away that he was dead.

Tenderly, he lifted the limp body and carried it over beside the fire where he examined it for wounds, but he found none. Then he saw the rope marks on the neck. He held the head in both his hands and moved it. The neck was not broken. Harley had been strangled with a rope.

"Aw, hell," Slocum moaned out loud. "Aw, partner. It was all my fault. I should've come out with you. I shouldn't have sent you out alone. Aw, hell. Aw, god-damn." Breathing heavily, he sat and looked into the face of the still warm body of his friend. "Harley," he said, "I know who done it. I seen them coming back to town with our horses. I know them, and I promise you, partner, I'll get every last one of the sons of bitches. I'll make them pay for this. I swear it to you. I'll make them pay if it's the last thing I do on this earth."

3

Back in the Booze Palace in Whizbang, Ace Carter and his cronies sat drinking whiskey. It was like a celebration. Morley Swenson poured another round, and then the bottle was empty. Carter looked over his shoulder toward the bar. "Hey, Dutch," he called out, "bring us another bottle of that good hooch over here." The barkeep reached under the counter for a bottle, then walked around the end of the bar to carry it to Carter's table. He set the bottle in the center of the table just as Morley was saying, "Imagine that damn fool drifter trying to tell us that him and his partner come in here looking for the law."

"What was that?" Dutch said.

"The cowboy that stole Tom Grant's horses," Morley said. "He tried to make us believe that him and his partner come into town looking for the law. Whoever heard of horse thieves riding into town looking for the law?"

"Them two that was in here earlier?" Dutch asked.

"Yeah," Morley said. "Them same two. They had Tom Grant's horses."

"They did," Dutch said.

"Yeah," said Morley. "They did have Tom Grant's horses."

"No," said Dutch. "I mean, they did come in and ask about the law."

"What was that?" Carter snapped. "Say that again."

"First thing they come in here," Dutch said, "they come up to the bar and said they'd found the marshal's office all locked up. They asked me where they could find the marshal. I told him he was out of town on business. They asked me did he have a deputy, and I told them no. I told them that Amos would be back day after tomorrow. That's right, ain't it? Day after tomorrow?"

The seven self-styled vigilantes suddenly became very quiet. They looked at one another, and the expressions on their faces were ones of guilt and fear.

"He wasn't lying," said one, at last breaking the heavy silence. "The son of a bitch wasn't lying."

"Shut up, Chapman," said Carter.

"But he said—"

"I said shut up," Carter roared.

"What's this all about?" Dutch asked.

"Never you mind," Carter said. "It's nothing. It don't concern you. Just go on about your business. Go on. Leave us alone here." Reluctantly, Dutch turned away and headed back toward the bar. Once or twice he looked back over at the seven men who were beginning to look to him like conspirators of some kind. "Okay," said Carter, with Dutch beyond ear shot, "so they asked after the law. So what? That don't mean nothing. They still stole Tom Grant's horses, didn't they? Hell, we got the horses right out front as evidence."

"Yeah," Morley said, but his face was still ashen. He didn't appear to have been convinced.

"If they was horse thieves like we figured," said Chilly Trumbull, "how come they brought them horses right back here to Whizbang? How come they gone looking for the law?"

"Goddamn it," said Carter, "I don't know how come. Maybe they stole them horses from ol' Tom and, thinking that they had killed him, maybe they come up with that story about hide hunters. Maybe they thought they could come in here and tell Amos that tall tale and get some kind of reward for turning in the very same horses they stole. Maybe—"

"Maybe they was telling the truth," said Trumbull. "Maybe we ought to tell Amos what we done soon as he gets back. The whole truth."

"Shut up," Carter said. "We got to stick together on this, and we got to stick to our story. We didn't do nothing wrong. Two strangers come into town, and they had Tom Grant's stoled horses. The law's out of town, and we done what had to be done. That's all. That's all except for one thing."

"What's that?" asked Morley.

"We got to find the other one and shut him up, too," Carter said. A somber silence settled over the whole group again for a few seconds before Carter continued. "Now, one of you go out there and take all them horses down to the stable. First thing in the morning, we'll get to tracking that other feller. What did he call himself? Slocum. He can't get far without his horse. Go on now."

Trumbull headed for the front door. "I'll get them," he said. Morley followed him, saying, "I'll give you a hand." In another minute, the two came running back in. Carter and the others shot them curious glances, as did Dutch from behind the bar. Running up to Carter and talking over his shoulder, Trumbull said in a harsh whisper, "It's gone. The Appaloosa. It's gone."

"What?" Carter roared.

"That Slocum's horse is gone," said Morley. "That fella we killed? He said his partner was still in town. Remember? He said he had took Slocum's horse out of town for a joke. Well, maybe he wasn't lying then neither. Maybe Slocum was still in town, and we brought him back his horse. Now he's took it, and there ain't no telling where he's at by now."

"Nor what he's going to do," said Trumbull. "He ain't going to like what he finds out at that camp."

The still, eerie silence took over once again. Carter poured himself another whiskey. He lifted the glass and downed it in a gulp, then poured himself another. Beads of sweat had broken out on his forehead.

"What are we going to do, Ace?" said Chapman.

"Stay calm," Carter said. "Don't no one go off half-cocked. You two go on ahead and take care of them horses, like I said. The rest of us will go on home, and we'll all gather up in front of Amos's office first thing in the morning, armed and ready to ride."

Up in the nearby hills, Slocum dug a grave. He dug it deep, and he wrapped the body of Harley Duggan, his partner, in his own blanket, for Harley's own blanket roll was on his horse in the possession of Ace Carter and the other six murderers. He laid the body in the grave carefully, almost tenderly, and then he sat on the pile of dirt there beside it. He took the hat off his head and wiped his brow. He looked up into the sky and stared for a long time.

"Whoever or whatever you are up there," he said at last, "you likely don't even know me. It ain't your fault. You never hear from me. My name's John Slocum. And this here is my partner, Harley Duggan. Harley was somewhat ornery, but he was a good man, and he didn't deserve what they done to him. I sure did like him a lot. He was a good friend to me. Now, I don't know what you think about it, but I mean to get the bastards that done it, and if you don't like that, I don't want you holding it against ol' Harley, even though I know that he'd be doing the same thing if it was me in that hole. Just treat him right. That's all I'm asking."

He stood up, took a deep breath, and started shoveling dirt back into the hole. There were tears in his eyes.

He built a small fire not far from the gravesite, heated up some beans and boiled some coffee. He ate the beans, then sat drinking coffee. He was thinking of the irony involved in Harley's death. He had told Harley to be careful getting involved with women, because women always got him into trouble. Then he had sent Harley out of town, and he himself had gotten involved with Millicent. Harley had been killed while Slocum was with Millicent. Then too, Harley had played a practical joke on Slocum, likely to get even with him for sending him out of town. He had taken Slocum's horse along, meaning to make Slocum walk out to the campsite. Had Harley not done that, likely the seven would have gotten Slocum, too.

For a brief moment, Slocum blamed Millicent for Harley's death. If she hadn't come over to him and drawn him into her place, none of this would have happened. But almost as soon as his mind framed this thought, he dismissed it. He knew that it wasn't fair. No, it was his own fault. He could have resisted the impulse to stay with her. He should have resisted. It was his own fault, and no one else's. He was to blame. He should have let Harley alone when Harley had first made a play for Millicent. Then everything would have been all right. Maybe he would have been at the camp when the seven arrived. Maybe he would be the dead one. Maybe he'd have taken a few with him. A few of the seven.

Then at last, he placed the blame once again where it rightly belonged. Harley's death was not Harley's fault, not Slocum's fault, not Millicent's. The blame was all on the shoulders of the self-righteous bastards who had done the cowardly and cold-blooded deed. The seven upright citizens who felt it was their duty to watch after their town while the marshal was away. Ace Carter was the main one, but the others, those willing to follow along with him, were guilty as well. Now, he told himself, since they had been willing, if not anxious, to follow Carter into wickedness, he would see to it that they followed him to hell.

It was time to quit musing and sulking. It was time to stop mourning for Harley. He had made a promise to Harley and to himself. He had even promised whatever up above ruled the heavens and the earth. It was time to go to work and keep that promise. He got up and cleaned his campsite, leaving as little trace of his presence as possible. He saddled the Appaloosa and mounted up. With one last look back at the new grave, he turned to ride away, but he did not ride toward Whizbang.

He knew that he could not just go riding into town and start shooting. He might get one or two of them that way, but if he tried to get them all like that, others in town would join with the seven, sure as hell. He knew as well that he could not ride his big Appaloosa back into Whizbang without someone taking immediate notice. Still, he had to find a way back into that town, preferably after dark. It was early morning, so he might have time to find himself another mount. He rode away from Whizbang.

Carter and the other six pulled up their horses at the site of the camp where they had found Harley Duggan the night before. None of the men were trackers, and the hoofprints and footprints around the camp were in such a jumble that even a good tracker would have had a problem making any sense out of them. Carter nudged his horse and rode over to the tree they had used. He looked at the ground beneath it. There was no body. Trumbull and Morley rode over, one on either side of Carter.

"It's gone," Trumbull said. "The body's gone."

"I can see that," said Carter. "I ain't blind."

"That means Slocum's been here," said Morley.

"Likely," Carter agreed.

"He knows what we done," Morley added.

"How would he know who done it?" Carter asked.

"He'll know," said Trumbull. "Who else could it have been?"

"Look around," Carter said. "See if we can find where he rode out of here on that big spotty-assed horse of his."

Slocum arrived at a lone house, a small rancher by the looks of it. He could see a corral with a number of horses in it. He rode slowly up toward the house, stopping a non-threatening distance away. Soon the front door was opened from inside, and a woman stepped out onto the porch. She was holding a rifle. Slocum waved and moved slowly forward. "Howdy, ma'am," he said. "Can I ride on in?"

"Come on," she said. "Slow. Keep your hands where I can see them."

Closer to the house, Slocum dismounted. He unbuckled his gun belt and took it off. Then he buckled it again and hung it over the saddlehorn. Stepping away from the big horse, he was unarmed. "Can I walk on in?" he asked.

"Come on," she said. Slocum walked up to the porch, leaving the Appaloosa on its own. "You got some nice horses over there," he said.

"You got a nice one yourself," she said.

"Yeah," he said, "but he's pretty obvious."

"You hiding from the law?" she asked.

"Not the law," he said. "I'd just like to be a little less noticeable for a spell. What I'd like to do is buy a horse and board my horse with you. I'll pay you for it. If anything happens that I don't come back, the horse is yours. I'll sign papers to that effect. He pulled some cash out of his jeans and held it out. She lowered the rifle.

"Pick a horse," she said. "Put yours in the corral. I'll be inside drawing up papers."

She turned and went inside. Slocum walked back to his horse and mounted up. He slung his gunbelt onto a shoulder. Inside the corral, he unsaddled the Appaloosa and gave it a slap on the rump. Then he walked around looking at the other horses there. He picked out a roan mare. She looked like a good one. She'd hold up well, and she was not particularly noticeable. He put his saddle on her and led her out of the corral and over to the porch. There he lapped the reins around the porch rail and stepped up onto the porch. He was about to knock on the door when he heard a voice call out from inside.

"Come on in."

Slocum stepped inside and took off his hat. The woman was sitting at a table with paper and pen. There was an empty chair across the table from her. "Sit down," she said, and he did. "You find a horse that suits you?" she asked. Slocum nodded toward the front.

"She's all saddled and waiting right at the porch," he said. "Little roan mare."

"I know her," the woman said. "What do you want to pay for her?"

Slocum laid some bills out on the table. The woman picked them up and counted them.

"She ain't worth that much," she said, and she started to peel off some bills.

"She is to me," said Slocum. "That's my offer."

The woman shrugged and laid the money down on the table in front of her.

"What's your name?" she asked.

"John Slocum," he said.

She wrote his name and filled in a few other items on the paper, then turned it for Slocum to read and sign. It was a bill of sale for the roan mare. He took note of her name on the paper: Halley Lawson. Then he signed it, folded it, and tucked it in his pocket. He pulled out some more money, this time in coins, and he laid that on the table.

"About the boarding," he said, "I think this will cover it."

The woman counted the coins and nodded.

"Mr. Slocum," she said, "it's a pleasure doing business with you. Whatever you're up to, I hope it all works out for you. I hope to see you again. That's a beautiful Appaloosa you got out there, but I don't want him. Not that way."

She stuck out her hand, and Slocum shook it. Then he put his hat on, touched the brim, and said, "Thank you, ma'am." He turned and left the house, and she walked to the door and watched as he mounted the roan mare, turned, and rode away.

"John Slocum," she said quietly. "I'll take care of your horse for you, and you come back to see me."

Halley Lawson was a good-looking woman, Slocum thought as he rode away from her house. He wondered if she lived alone and worked those horses alone or if there was a Mr. Lawson around somewhere. She had written her name on the paper, "Halley Lawson." That was all. Usually a married woman would sign her name with the

"Mrs." written in front of it, usually even with her husband's first name there, too. And he had seen no sign of a bunkhouse or any other evidence of hired hands.

It was a rough life and a rugged place for a woman alone, but Halley Lawson had the look of a woman who could handle it. She looked tough, although the toughness did not spoil her good looks. That was unusual, and Slocum liked that combination in a woman. If he had not had such urgent business to take care of, he thought, he would have looked for some excuse to hang around longer. Maybe she had some work that needed doing, and he could have offered his help. Maybe—

He felt guilty. Harley was fresh in the ground because of his dallying, and here he was thinking of another woman. He tried to put Halley Lawson out of his mind and concentrate on Ace Carter and the other six. It wasn't easy, but he kept trying.

"Ace," said Morley, "I ain't for sure, but I think he rode out this way."

Carter rode over to where Morley was following a set of tracks that left the campsite. "Well, I ain't no tracker either," he said, "but I bet you're right. They leave the camp alone and go off thataway, not back toward town. Let's try them, boys. The sooner we get that bastard, the safer we are."

He whipped up his mount, riding after the tracks, and the other six rode after him. Soon, however, he had to slow the pace, realizing that the tracks led off for some distance, and they would wear out their horses unless they eased up. Morley rode up beside Carter. "He's run off, Ace," he said. "Reckon we ought to just let well enough alone?"

"We ain't sure this is him, Morley," Carter said. "And if it is him, we ain't sure what he's up to. We'll just keep after them till we are sure."

The tracks led the seven into the foothills, and then they vanished.

"Damn," Carter said. "This trail's too rocky. I've lost the goddamn tracks."

"There's only one way to go from here," Trumbull said. "At least for a while."

They continued on the trail to a place where the ground leveled off again. Morley said, "Looky here. Here's the tracks again."

But Carter did not look. He was looking at something else. A fresh mound of dirt. Slowly the others noticed him and saw what he was staring at. Trumbull rode over by his side.

"What're you thinking, Ace?" he asked.

"I'm thinking that Slocum come up here to bury his pard," Carter said.

"Maybe he did," said Trumbull. "Let's see where his tracks lead from here."

"First," said Carter, "let's make sure we're following the right tracks."

"What do you mean, Ace?" Trumbull said.

"Only one way I know to make sure we're following the right tracks," Carter said.

The other five had all ridden up close by this time and were listening to what Carter had to say. Morley said, "You mean—"

"Dig it up," said Carter. "Dig it up. If it's Slocum's pard in there, then we know we're following Slocum. Dig it up."

4

Hesitantly, at the urging of Ace Carter, two men dug into the fresh grave, fussing and complaining the whole time. The sun was hot already in the sky, and the air was hot and dry. The two diggers were soon soaked with sweat. The other five men, including Carter, either sat on horseback or stood and watched with somber faces.

"Goddamn," said one digger, "whoever he was, he sure planted him deep." At last they reached the body. "It's all wrapped up," the digger said.

"Well, unwrap it," said Carter. "Whoever's in there ain't going to bite you. He's dead."

Reluctantly, the man knelt in the hole, his face wrinkled in disgust, and gingerly, he took hold of the edge of the blanket between a finger and thumb. He pulled at the blanket until all present could see the face and the scarred neck.

"It's him, all right," the man said with a shudder. The other digger shuddered as well. Carter took a long look from atop his horse, as if he were studying the remains, trying to memorize them. Then, "Let's go," he said. "We've got to catch up with his goddamn funeral director."

"We going to leave him just like that?" asked Trumbull.

"He don't care," Carter said, and he turned his horse and continued to follow the hoofprints of the big Appaloosa. The others hurried to fall in behind him. Trumbull

32

took a last look at the opened grave. Then he too rode on.
An hour or so later they lost the tracks once more, and
they milled around in circles trying to pick them up again.
They had no luck.

"The ground's too hard here," Morley said. "We've lost
him. Might as well turn back."

"We'll just have to make a guess," said Carter, ignoring
Morley. He pointed ahead. "That way makes most sense."

They rode on. It was past noon when they stopped to
rest their horses. They were hot and they were hungry.
They had not planned on a long ride, and they were becoming irritable. "He's long gone," said Morley. "Hell,
he's left the damn country. We ain't never going to see
him again. I say we turn around and go home."

"Morley's right," said another. "Let's head back."

"We ain't sure about that," said Carter. "We got to be sure."

Slocum topped a rise on the little roan, and he saw a gathering of men down below him and a distance ahead. He
quickly halted the little horse and backed her up. Then he
rode into the hills off to his left. He found a place where
he could dismount, hide the horse, and settle himself down
snug behind a large boulder. He took a pair of binoculars
out of his saddlebag and studied the gang down below and
ahead. Right away, he recognized Ace Carter. He looked
carefully at each man, studied each face. He wanted to be
sure he would never forget any one of those seven men.
He meant to kill them all for what they had done to Harley.

He put away the spy glasses and took out his Winchester. Cranking a shell into the chamber, he settled down
again against the big rock. He made himself comfortable
and took careful aim, but it was a long shot. Too long, he
knew. He knew that he couldn't get all seven men like
this. He would be lucky to hit even one. But he didn't
want to face them like this anyhow. Seven to one. He
couldn't just ride into them shooting. Perhaps, he thought,
a shot down among them would scare them all back to
Whizbang. That was where he really wanted them. In
Whizbang they would separate. They would go to their

individual homes and individual jobs. He could wait a while, let them relax, then slip up on them one at a time.

He sighted in on Carter and squeezed the trigger.

Carter felt something tear at his left shoulder, and he saw the blood fly even before he heard the distant rifle report. Spinning and falling to a sitting position on the ground, he yelped and grabbed at the ragged bloody spot on his shoulder. He felt a mixture of torn cloth, torn flesh, and hot, sticky blood.

"Goddamn," shouted Morley.

"Where'd that come from?" asked Trumbull.

"What was it?" another said.

"I been shot," Carter said.

"Who done it?" said one.

"It's that Slocum," said another. "Where the hell is he?"

Carter still sat down clutching his wound. He watched as the sticky blood oozed between his fingers. His face was white as if he were in shock.

"Somebody help me here," he said. "I'm hurt." The other five men all had guns in their hands, all looked wildly around. Morley ran to his horse and pulled out a rifle.

"You stupids," he said. "Six-guns won't do no good. Get your rifles."

Trumbull looked ahead to the far hills. "He's up there," he said. "Rifles won't even do us any good. Not from here. That was a hell of a shot he made."

"A lucky shot," said Morley. "That's all."

"Damn it," said Carter. "I'm bleeding here."

A bullet kicked up dust just in front of Morley. He yelped and jumped, and then he heard the sound of the shot.

"Shit," he said. "Well, sit there and bleed then. I'm going back." He mounted up as quickly as his skittish horse would allow, turned it, lashed at it, and rode hard back the way they had come. Others followed him. Trumbull knelt beside the whimpering Carter.

"Come on," he said. "Let's get mounted. I'll help you."

"I'm bleeding," said Carter.

"If we don't get out of here," said Trumbull, "we'll both

be dead. Come on now. We get a safe distance away from here, we'll tend to that wound. Come on."

He managed to get the whimpering Carter to his feet and onto his horse. Then as he was turning to mount his own, another bullet kicked up dust. Carter kicked his horse in the sides and rode off after the others. Trumbull's horse bolted, causing Trumbull to fall over onto his back, landing hard in the dirt.

"Hey," he said, scampering to his feet. "Come back." He ran a few steps after the skittish horse, saw that it was futile, and turned back to look after Carter.

"Ace!" he yelled. "Come back. I'm afoot here. Ace!"

But Ace Carter was thinking only of his own skin. He didn't even bother looking back over his shoulder as he fled. Trumbull stared after him, unbelieving for a moment. Then the severity of his situation settled in his brain. He turned and looked back toward the hills where the shots had come from. He was alone. He was on foot. His rifle was with his runaway horse, so he was armed only with a six-gun. He had no food or water, and the sun was beating down on him. Of course, he knew that food and water would not be a real worry, not for long, for the gunman in the hills was surely Slocum, and Slocum would have a horse, and Slocum would be riding down after him. Desperate, Trumbull looked after Carter once more and screamed as loud as he could.

"Ace! Come back! Don't leave me here!"

Slocum rode the little mare slowly. There was no hurry. The six men on horseback would ride back to Whizbang, and he would find them all there. The seventh man, the one who had lost his horse, would not move anywhere very quickly. Slocum would catch him easily. He lost sight of the man once or twice due to the rising and falling landscape, but that didn't worry him either. The man had no place to go. He wouldn't run for the hills, for that was where Slocum was riding from. He watched the man, still looking very small some distance ahead, run, stagger, and fall, then get up and run again. Finally the man quit run-

ning. He walked. He walked generally toward Whizbang.
Slocum did not increase his pace.

Now and then Trumbull would look back over his shoulder to see the hellish rider coming after him. He wondered
what Slocum was up to. He was moving so slowly. It
would be easy for him to catch up and finish Trumbull
off. Trumbull knew that. So why was he moving so
slowly? He was gaining a little at a time, decreasing the
distance between them. So why, Trumbull suddenly asked
himself, was he still fleeing? He knew that there was no
way he could outdistance Slocum. He was accomplishing
nothing. He was only wearing himself out. His breathing
was rapid and short due to his exertion, and the heavy
panting was drying out his throat and mouth. He decided
that he would stop and face Slocum. Bring an end to this.
Why not?

Slocum saw that the man had stopped moving, had instead
turned to face him. Still he walked the roan. The distance
was being closed now faster than before, but still not
quickly. The man ahead sat down to wait. He had given
up. Abandoned by his own *compadres*, he didn't have a
chance, and he obviously knew it. Slocum rode to within
an easy rifle shot and stopped. The man stood up and drew
out his revolver. Slocum slipped his Winchester out of its
scabbard and leveled it at the man.

"Throw that six-gun away," he said, "or I'll drop you
from here."

Trumbull hesitated a moment, then tossed the revolver
away. Slocum lowered his Winchester and rode on in. A
few feet from Trumbull, he stopped. Sitting in the saddle,
he looked down at the wretched man.

"Well, go on," Trumbull said defiantly. "Get it over with."

"Not just yet," said Slocum. "Why'd you do it?"

"What?" said Trumbull.

"What did Harley do to make you kill him like that?"
Slocum said. "I want to know."

"He had Tom Grant's horses," Trumbull said. "Morley

saw them. Ace said that you two must be the ones that nearly killed old Tom Grant and stole his horses. We rode out to your camp, but you weren't there. We were just trying to make him tell us where you were. That's all."

"How'd you do it?" Slocum asked.

Trumbull tried to swallow, but there was nothing in his dry mouth. He gulped air.

"I didn't do it," he said. "It was Chunk Hedley threw the rope over the tree limb. They put the noose around his neck and just pulled it tight, meaning to make him talk. They pulled a little too much, I guess. We never meant to kill him. It just happened. That's all."

"What did he tell you about the horses?" Slocum asked.

"He said that you all got them off of some hide hunters that attacked your camp," said Trumbull.

"Did he also tell you that we rode into your goddamn town looking for the law to report the whole thing?" Slocum asked.

"Well, yeah," said Trumbull. "He did, but Ace said he was lying about that."

"There's you and Ace Carter," Slocum said. "What are the others' names?"

"Morley," said Trumbull. "Morley Swenson. Chunk Hedley. Gary Chapman. Doby Barber, and then there's Sammy Cain. That's all."

"That's seven," said Slocum. "What kind of men are you? Seven men to torture one man to death? Hell, you didn't even know you had the right man. Everything Harley told you was true."

"Ace said he was lying," Trumbull stammered.

"Does Ace do all the thinking for the whole town?" Slocum snapped. "Say them names again. Just the last names."

"Carter, Swenson, Chapman, Hedley, Barber, Cain," said Trumbull. "And me, I'm Trumbull."

Slocum made Trumbull repeat the names again several times until he had them memorized. At last the seven names were burned into his brain. They would never leave it, at least not until all seven men were dead. He slipped the Winchester back into its sheath and swung down off his horse.

"Go pick up your six-gun," he said.

"What?" said Trumbull.

"You heard me," said Slocum. "Pick it up."

Trumbull edged toward the gun, looking quickly from Slocum to the weapon and back again. At last he stood next to it. He leaned over, eyes on Slocum. He had to glance down to keep from picking up only a handful of dirt, but he looked quickly back at Slocum. Trumbull had his hand on the revolver's butt. Slocum was just standing straight, his own Colt still holstered. Trumbull gripped the revolver. Slowly he straightened up. He held the weapon down by his side.

"I ain't a murderer," Slocum said. "Your gun's in your hand. Mine's holstered. That's more than fair. Make your play."

"No," said Trumbull. "Wait a minute. If you don't mean to murder me, then I won't fight. I won't fight you. Then you can't kill me. Not without murdering me. I won't fight."

"Would you rather die slow out here?" Slocum asked. He walked over to the roan and took a canteen off the saddle. He uncorked it and started to pour the water out on the ground. "If you're lucky, you might kill me," he said. "Then you'd have my horse and what's left of this water."

Trumbull watched the water run out onto the ground until he could stand it no longer.

"No!" he shouted, and he raised his revovler to shoot. He didn't even have time to cock it. Slocum's own Colt was out and spitting lead too fast. One slug slammed into Trumbull's chest. A second tore into his throat. He staggered, gagged, rocked on his feet back and forth, then fell over on his back and lay still. Slocum walked over to check. Trumbull was dead.

"That's one, ol' pard," he said out loud. "Six to go."

He ejected the two spent shells from the cylinder and reloaded the Colt. Then he walked back to the roan, mounted her, and rode on toward Whizbang without looking back.

Let the buzzards and coyotes have a feast, he thought, desert rats, anything that likes dead and rotting flesh.

Carter and the other five had gone far enough. They thought it was safe at last to stop and rest. Besides, they had run their horses so far and so fast that the more prudent among them knew they would kill the animals if they didn't stop and allow them to rest. Carter pulled off his jacket and shirt and found that his wound had stopped bleeding. It was superficial after all, a flesh wound. He realized that he had panicked. He knew, too, that he had abandoned poor Chilly Trumbull, assuring his death. He felt a pang of guilt, but he would keep that to himself. It was a small thing compared to what they had done to the cowboy—if he had really been innocent, and it was looking more that way all the time.

"How's your shoulder?" Chunk Hedley asked.

"Huh?" said Carter, looking up quickly. "Oh. It's all right. It'll heal. A scratch, that's all. Just a scratch."

"Say," Doby Barber asked. "Where's Chilly? I don't see Chilly."

Carter looked around as if he had no idea, as if the fact that Trumbull was missing from their ranks was a complete surprise to him. The pang of guilt had passed rather easily.

"Why, he was right behind me when we rode out," he said. "Something must have happened to him."

"Slocum got him," said Morley Swenson.

"You don't know that for sure," Carter said. "Maybe it was something else. Maybe his horse went lame or something."

"No," Swenson said. "Slocum got him. He's going to get the rest of us, too. One at a time. He'll get us all. We're all dead men."

"Bullshit," said Hedley. "He fired them shots just to throw us off his trail. That's all. Now we're headed back, he's on his way out of the country. He don't want no part of what his partner got. He's running."

"It didn't seem to me like he was running," Sammy

Cain said. "Looks to me like we're the ones running."

"Laying in ambush to turn back a posse is one thing," Hedley said. "Coming to face us direct in Whizbang is something else entire. Hell, he's on his way to Californee. Mark my words. We seen the last of that son of a bitch, all right."

"Then where's Chilly?" said Cain. "Where the hell is he? If he was riding along right behind Ace, how come he ain't right here now with the rest of us?"

"He'll be coming along any time now," said Hedley. "You'll see."

"I can't even see him back there anywhere," Cain said. "If he was still a coming, we ought to be able to see him back there. It's flat as a pancake for miles, and I don't see no sign of him."

"If you're so worried about Chilly," Carter said, "ride back and look for him."

"By myself?" Cain asked.

"Then shut up about it," said Carter.

Just then, Barber happened to glance over to see Chapman hunkered down on the far side of his horse as if he were hiding something. Barber moved around a little and looked more closely, and then he could see that Chapman was eating something.

"Hey," Barber said. "What you got there?"

"It's mine," said Chapman.

"He's got biscuits," said Barber.

"No," Chapman said. "Just one. It's mine."

Barber rushed over to Chapman's horse and reached into a saddlebag. Chapman shoved him away.

"Stay out of there," he said. "That's mine."

"Why do you want me to stay out if you ain't got no more biscuits in there?" Barber said. He started scuffling with Chapman. Soon Hedley and Cain joined in and held Chapman back. Barber dug into the bag and found a stash of biscuits.

"Look here," he said. "The bastard was holding out on us." He started tossing biscuits around to each of the others. Chapman stopped struggling, and Hedley and Cain released him. He turned his back, walked away a few steps, then sat down.

"You goddamn thieves," he said.

"Yeah?" said Hedley. "And you're a no-good, tightwad son of a bitch to hold out like that on your friends."

"Some friends," Chapman said. "You ain't my friends. Look what you got me into. We killed an innocent man, didn't we? Didn't we? And now his buddy's coming after us. And he's some kind of a gunfighter, too. He's already killed Chilly, and he'll kill us all before he quits."

"What do you mean we got you into it?" Hedley said. "We all went into it together. Nobody twisted your damn arm. You were as anxious to go after them two cowboys as any of the rest of us."

"You're the one that strung him up," Chapman said.

"Don't you try to lay it all off on me, you little shit," said Hedley. "We was just trying to make him talk. That's all."

"How could he talk when you was choking him?" Chapman said. "You're sadistic. That's what you are."

"What the hell does that mean?" Hedley asked.

"Shut up!" Carter suddenly shouted. With the realization that his wound was but slight, he had regained his boisterous and authoritative manner. "The whole thing was my idea," he went on. "I admit that. I own up to it, but all of you went along without any complaints that I can recall. Now, goddamn it, we can't start fighting among ourselves here. We all got to stick together."

"You think that Slocum's lit out of here?" Morley asked.

"Slocum's coming after us," said Carter. "That's one thing for damn sure."

5

Grimly, Slocum followed after the surviving six murderers, but he did not rush himself. He was in no hurry. One killing a day was plenty for him. Besides, he figured the longer he dragged it out the more the bastards would suffer. And he wanted them to suffer. They had sure made Harley suffer. He wished that he could get the horrible image of Harley's body out of his mind, but he could not, and then he finally decided that maybe it was best that way, at least until he had killed the other six murderers. That awful and painful image would keep him determined, keep him going. It would keep him cold and hard. That was the way it had to be.

He got within eyeshot of them, and he slowed his pace even more. He was pretty sure they had not yet seen him, and he wanted to keep it that way for a while. The day was getting short, so he made himself a cold camp in the hills looking down on the gang below. He took out his looking glasses again to study them, and he could see easily that there was unrest among them. That was good, he thought. Let them make things even worse for themselves. As he watched, five of the men, including Ace Carter, mounted their horses and headed on toward Whizbang.

One stayed behind. He sat alone with his back to the rest. His horse grazed casually nearby. This one must have had a serious falling out with the others. Why else would he have stayed on alone? The others rode on and left the loner to himself. They would make it on into town, all right, but their horses would never be quite the same. Slocum thought them a bunch of fools, but then, anyone who would do what they had done to Harley couldn't be expected to treat horses right.

Chapman sat cross-legged on the ground, his arms crossed over his chest, his back to the others, a hard pout set on his face. He looked over his shoulder once as the others mounted their horses to continue the ride back to town, but when one looked in his direction, he snapped his head back around. Hedley hesitated and called back to him. "Gary," he said, "you coming?" Chapman did not answer. "Fuck you then," Hedley said, and he kicked his horse to race after the rest.

"Fuck you, too," said Chapman, but he did not say it out loud. He muttered it as if to himself. "You shit. Bunch of shits."

When they were all nearly out of sight, Chapman at last stood up. He stared hard after them for a long moment. Then he walked over to his horse and found one last biscuit in the bag. He pulled it out and began gnawing at it. After a few seconds, he looked nervously around himself. As far as he could tell, he was alone. It was quiet and still. There was no sign of human life that he could see.

"Huh," he said out loud, "ain't no one coming after us. Ain't no one out here even. I'm all right. Yeah. I'm all right." He gnawed some more biscuit, but his belly started craving grease, and he had no meat. He was also thinking of whiskey. He wanted a steak and some good whiskey. "I better start on back, though," he said, still out loud and talking to himself. "I better go. It'll get dark on me if I don't hurry on up." He glanced again toward the hills in the background from where the shots had come. He wondered about Trumbull. Holding what was left of the biscuit in his mouth, he quickly mounted his horse and started riding after Carter and the others.

He rode for a distance quickly, then slowed down, walking his horse. He went on for a while like that before he looked back over his shoulder. He stopped, his mouth hanging open. Far behind, he thought he saw a horse and rider coming at him as if through a mist. He waited, and the figure came closer, loomed slightly larger. Chapman urged his tired horse ahead faster. He rode hard, but when he looked back, he still saw the mysterious figure coming behind him. He lashed at the poor animal, lashed and kicked and raced ahead. He thought then that he should have gone on with the others, no matter how he had felt about them at the time. It had only been his foolish pride that had kept him behind and put him in this danger. He should have known better. He should have used better judgment.

He lashed harder, and his horse stumbled, throwing him over its head. He screamed as he flew through the air, landed hard, and then rolled on the hard dirt. When he finally sat up and shook his head clear from the rough tumble, he saw that his horse was back up on its feet, but even he could tell that it would go no more. He looked back and saw the ominous figure coming ever closer. He saw it as the figure of death itself. He struggled up onto his own feet and hurried back to the horse, but he was walking with a limp. The fall had hurt his leg. He whimpered as he pulled the rifle out of its scabbard. He looked around quickly for cover, and it was only then that he realized he had taken his fall right near the ghastly open grave that had earlier been desecrated by him and the others.

He shuddered, but he saw no cover save the mound of dirt they had piled up there by the grave, so he ran over, still limping, and settled himself down on the far side of the mound from the approaching rider. In his peripheral vision he could see the exposed body in the hole to his left. Looking ahead again, he could still see the figure of death moving slowly toward him, and it still appeared as if through a mist or a haze. In desperation, he took aim and squeezed off a round. The shot sounded like an explosion in the silence, and it made his ears ring. He looked ahead and squinted, and the relentless figure was still moving steadily, still coming at him. His whimpering increased until it had almost become a sobbing. He fired again, but he knew as he fired that his shot was wild and useless.

Slocum stopped. He steadied the roan until it stood stark still. He studied the scene ahead for a moment, then pulled out his Winchester and cranked a shell into the chamber. He had thought that one killing a day was enough, but this man was forcing the issue. Well, so be it. Raising the rifle to his shoulder, he aimed at the mound of dirt ahead and fired. Quickly he levered another round into the chamber and fired again, and again. He knew he would not hit the man, unless with a lucky shot, but he also knew that he would cause a panic, and that would be just about as effective.

Dirt was kicked into Chapman's face with the first shot. He whirled around and pressed his back against the mound and felt the dirt from the second and third shots flick into the hair on top of his head. His whimpering grew louder and faster. In a panic, he jumped to his feet and ran for his horse. Tired or not, it would have to run. He would ride it to death if need be. Another shot rang out and dirt was kicked up between his feet. He jumped and screamed. In a few more running strides, he reached the horse, and he mounted quickly. He kicked and lashed at it, and it turned to make a last valiant effort. Then another shot rang out as Chapman felt the hot slug tear into his back.

"Oh no," he whined. "Oh no."

He tried to hang on as the horse began to run. He tried to control the horse, but he was only just sitting there. He was as useless as a sack of grain. His fingers no longer gripped the reins. His legs no longer pressed against the horse's sides. He couldn't tell if his feet were in the stirrups or not. He wasn't even really sitting in the saddle. It was more like someone had just placed him there. He

knew he was going to fall. His brain told him to stop the
horse, but his body refused to respond. He reeled in the
saddle. At last he fell.

When he hit the ground, he hit hard, and it hurt. It hurt
like hell, but then suddenly the hurting stopped. He lay
flat on his back staring straight up into the sky. A buzzard
circled above, and it made him want to shiver. The shiver
stayed inside. His body refused to move. He had no control and no feeling. He was battered and broken, and he
was actually surprised to find himself still alive. He was
numb, not hurting, but his mouth and throat were parched.
He thought of water. He knew that the mysterious death
figure coming out of the mist had shot him, and he wondered if the man would come over and finish the job or
just let him die slowly. He no longer knew where his rifle
was. It didn't matter. He figured that his revolver was at
his side, but he couldn't make his arm move to reach for
it.

Slocum realized as he drew nearer what the mound of dirt
was, where it had come from. He rode in quickly then,
and found that his worst fears were true. The bastards, he
said to himself. The dirty sons of bitches. They had actually dug up Harley's grave. Pulling the little roan to a
quick stop, he dismounted and raced to the grave's side.
Looking down, he could see Harley's exposed face. He
dropped down into the open grave and pulled the blanket
back around the face. Then with his bare hands, he started
scraping the dirt back into the grave.

Chapman could barely roll his eyes, but he saw the man
walking toward him where he lay. He tried to speak, but
his throat was so dry and parched that only a harsh rasping
sound came out. Slocum walked up close and looked down
on him.

"Not quite dead yet, huh?" he said.

Chapman rasped out a noise.

"I found what you did over there," Slocum said. "It
wasn't enough that you murdered my partner, was it? Tor-

tured him to death? That wasn't enough. You came out here and dug up his grave. Why the hell did you do that?" Chapman breathed out a heavy rasping sound. Slocum knelt beside him. "Can't talk, huh?" Slocum said. "Throat dry? Have some of the dirt you dug out of Harley's grave."

He raised a closed fist up over Chapman's face, and as he slowly opened it, dirt ran out and down into Chapman's already tortured dry mouth. Chapman convulsed with gags and coughs. He tried to spit, but he could not. His hand empty of dirt, Slocum stood again. He turned to face the grave.

"That's two down, pard," he said. "Five to go."

He walked back toward the roan with Chapman still alive, still coughing and convulsing. He mounted up and rode away and left the son of a bitch like that. He wouldn't last long.

Slocum rode right into Whizbang, right down the middle of the main street. He rode straight to the town marshal's office, and this time he found it open. He tied his horse to the rail and walked into the office. A big man with a handlebar mustache looked up from behind the desk.

"You the marshal?" Slocum asked.

"That's right," the man said. "Amos Foss. What can I do for you?"

"I wish you'd have been here whenever me and my partner rode into town," Slocum said. "I ain't sure what you can do now."

"You want to tell me just what the hell you're talking about?" asked Foss.

"Yeah," Slocum said. "I'll give it a shot."

Foss stood up and indicated a chair. "Sit down," he said, and Slocum did. "Coffee?"

"Sure," said Slocum. "Thanks."

Foss poured two cups, gave one to Slocum and took the other back around to the other side of his desk and sat down again. He looked up and into Slocum's face, as if to say that he was ready to hear the tale, whatever it might be.

"My name's Slocum," Slocum said. "Me and my partner Harley Duggan run into a little trouble back down the trail. We were set on by four men, hide hunters, by the looks of them. We killed them, all four. We were headed this way, so we brought their horses in. Meant to tell you what happened, and ask your advice on what to do with the horses. But you weren't here. We decided to wait. I sent Harley on out of town to make us a camp. When I got out there later, I found him killed. Strangled with a rope.

"It seems that some of your upstanding citizens had seen Harley taking those horses back out of town and decided that me and Harley had stole them from some fellow named Tom Grant."

"Grant had some horses stole, all right," said Foss nodding his head. "They've been recovered. They're down at the stable right now."

"These citizens," Slocum continued, "rode out to the camp site and put a noose around Harley's neck. They strung him up and strangled him, trying to get him to tell them where I was at. Hell, he didn't even know except that I was still in town. He told them that, too, but they killed him just the same."

"How do you know all that if you were in town?" Foss asked.

"One of them told me the whole story," said Slocum. "Name of Trumbull. Right before I killed him."

"You killed Trumbull?" Foss asked.

"Deader'n hell," said Slocum. "There were seven of them, and they found my trail. Along the way they found where I'd buried Harley, and they dug him up again. Anyhow, they caught up with me, but I scared them off with a couple of shots. One of them nicked Carter. Ace Carter. He's the leader of the pack. They all run off, but Trumbull lost his horse. I faced him alone, and he confessed the whole thing to me. Then he went for his gun, and I killed him."

"There were no witnesses to this killing, I take it," Foss said.

"No witnesses," said Slocum. "I followed the others, and while I was watching them, they seemed to get into it with each other while they were taking a rest. When they mounted up to ride on, one of them stayed behind alone. I went after him. When he noticed me behind him, he started shooting a rifle at me. I shot back."

"You killed him, too?" Foss said.

"That's right," said Slocum. "I don't know his name."

"It was probably Gary Chapman," Foss said. "He's not anywhere around. I knew something was going on around here, but I haven't been able to get anything out of anybody. I figured Ace Carter was behind it somewhere."

"It was him all right," Slocum said.

"I want you to do something for me, Slocum," said Foss. "I want you to ride out to the Grant place with me. The doc tells me that old Tom is doing a bit better now, and he could likely take one look at you and tell me whether you were one of the ones that nearly killed him and stole his horses. That'll give us a starting place in this mess. Will you ride out with me?"

"I will," Slocum said.

It wasn't a long ride, and they found Tom Grant sitting up in bed. Standing at the bedside, Amos Foss said, "Tom, this is John Slocum."

"Howdy, Slocum," said Grant. "Sorry I can't get up."

"From what I hear, Mr. Grant," Slocum said, "you're lucky to be sitting up and talking."

"Yeah," said Grant. "I reckon so."

"We got your horses, Tom," Foss said. "They're in the stable in town. I'll send them out sometime tomorrow."

"Thank you, Amos," said Grant. "What about those bastards that did this to me?"

"Well, now," said Foss, "I don't rightly know about them. They—Tom, have you ever met Mr. Slocum here before today?"

"Can't say that I have," Grant said. "Am I supposed to have?"

"No," said Foss. "That's all right. Did you see the men that attacked you?"

"Seen them good," said Grant. "Four of them it was. Nasty-looking bunch. I took them to be hide hunters down on their luck."

"Did you hear any names called?" Foss asked.

"Well, now, let me see," Grant said.

"Ned?" said Slocum.

"Yeah," said Grant. "Yeah. One of them was called Ned. That's right. How'd you know?"

"How about Joseph?" said Slocum.

"Yes sir," said Grant. "There was a Joseph. Weasly little bastard he was."

"They're dead," Slocum said. "All four of them."

"Who killed them?" asked Grant.

"I did," Slocum said. "Me and my partner. We brought your horses back to town after that."

"Well, I sure do thank you for that," Grant said. "All dead and my horses back, too. Thank you."

"The first part of your story's confirmed," Foss said as he and Slocum stepped down off the porch of Tom Grant's ranch house. "Now we have to deal with the rest of it."

"The rest of it happened just like I told you," said Slocum. "Carter and his gang saw Harley with the horses and figured that me and him was the thieves. They found him alone and tortured him to death. Then they went after me. I killed two of them. I mean to kill the other five before I quit."

"Now, hold on, Slocum," Foss said. "I can't let you run around Whizbang killing folks. Not even if what you're telling me is true. I need some time to get to the bottom of this."

"There's nothing to get to," Slocum said. "They killed Harley and then dug up his grave. I mean to kill them. All of them."

"If you kill anyone in my town," Foss said, "I'll arrest you for murder."

"It won't be murder," said Slocum, "but they'll be just as dead."

"Slocum, let the law handle this," Foss said. "If we can prove what they did, they'll hang for murder."

"Yeah?" Slocum said. "And what if you can't prove it? They all get away clean? I ain't taking that chance. Harley was my partner. They strung him up and killed him slow. Then they went and dug up his grave. Why the hell did they do a thing like that? You tell me, if you was in my place, what would you do? Wait for the law and hope they could prove it? Would you?"

"I'd do the same as you, Slocum," said Foss, "but right here and now, I'm representing the law, and I got to tell you to leave it alone and let me deal with it."

"Well, you're wasting your breath," Slocum said. "I mean to kill them. That's all I can say."

6

Amos Foss found Ace Carter drinking whiskey in the Booze Palace. It was early in the day for Carter to be drinking so much, and Foss took notice of that fact. He walked over to Carter's table.

"Mind if I join you, Ace?" he asked.

"Help yourself," Carter said, his voice surly.

"Why so friendly?" Foss asked.

"Aw, hell, Amos," Carter said, "I didn't mean nothing by it. I just got a lot of things on my mind is all. Sit down. Have a drink on the house."

"Just coffee," Foss said. "It's a little early for me."

"Hey, Dutch," Carter called out. "Cup of coffee for the marshal here."

"Coming right up," Dutch said.

"I hear there was a little excitement in town while I was away," Foss said casually.

"Oh yeah?" said Carter. "What's that? What'd you hear?"

Dutch brought the coffee and set it on the table in front of Foss.

"Thanks," said Foss.

"Anytime, Amos," Dutch said. He walked back to the bar. Foss took a tentative sip of the hot coffee and put the cup back down.

"Couple of cowboys brought in Tom Grant's horses that were stole," said Foss.

"Oh, yeah," said Carter. "That. Yeah. Them horses is down in the stable. That was lucky for old Tom. Yeah, I knew about that."

"There's a little more to the story," said Foss. Carter slugged down the whiskey in his glass and poured himself another. He did not look at Foss when he next spoke.

"What else you hear?" he asked.

"Some of the boys figured that the two cowhands stole the horses," Foss said. "They rode out where the strangers were camped. Only found one of them. They strung him up to a tree trying to make him talk. They might not have meant to do it, but they killed him."

"Naw," said Carter, incredulous. "Who'd you hear that from?"

"Then they went hunting the other feller," Foss continued. "They found him all right, but he killed two of them. Seems it was Trumbull and Chapman."

"Chilly and Gary?" said Carter. "Chilly and Gary killed? I can't hardly believe it. Come to think on it, though, I ain't seen either one of them around town for a spell."

"Yeah," said Foss. "Seems like there were seven altogether. Seven that killed the cowboy. His partner means to kill the other five before he quits. It would be a good thing if those five were to turn themselves in to me before that happens. Be a real good thing. I hate to see a bloodbath around here."

"Yeah," said Carter. "I can see your point. I guess that would be the best thing for them five to do—before that drifter catches up to them. Say, who'd you hear all this from, anyway?"

"I heard it," said Foss. "That's enough for now. I heard more, too."

"Yeah?" said Carter.

"I heard you were the leader of the mob," Foss said.

"That's crazy," Carter snapped. "What lying son of a bitch said that?"

"Never mind that part," Foss said.

"You going to arrest me?" said Carter defiantly. "You got any proof of them outrageous allegations?"

"No," Foss said. "I ain't going to arrest you. Not just yet anyhow. And, no, I ain't got proof. Just stories."

"You ain't even got no bodies," said Carter. "Have you? You got bodies?"

"No," Foss said. "I got no bodies. Got no proof. I do know one thing for sure though."

"What's that?" Carter asked.

"I know the cowboys didn't steal Tom's horses," said Foss. "Tom came around, and I went out to see him. He said four hide hunters stole the horses. Seems like the cowboys claimed they got the horses off four hide hunters. You hear that part of the story? Well, anyhow, they were telling the truth about that." He took a final sip of coffee and then stood up. "It sure would be better for those five men if they were to give themselves up to me," he said. Then he left the saloon.

"Dutch," Carter shouted. "Watch after things here. I got something to do."

He got up out of his chair and headed for the door. He stood there in the doorway for a moment and watched Foss walk toward his office. Then he went outside and headed for the boot shop of Morley Swenson. He walked fast, but he was reeling a little from all the early day whiskey he had consumed. Bursting into the boot shop, he saw that Swenson was with a customer.

"Morley," he said, heading for the shop's back room, "we need to talk."

He shoved open the door to the back room.

"In a minute, Ace," Swenson said.

"Right now," said Carter.

Swenson looked at his customer.

"Just try them on till you're satisfied," he said. "I'll be right back with you." He followed Carter into the back room. "What?" he said. "I have a customer out there."

"This is more important," said Carter. "I just had a talk with Amos Foss, and he knows everything."

"What?" Swenson said.

"He knows everything," said Carter, "but he ain't got no proof. All we got to do is keep our yaps shut, and we'll be all right. Just don't let any of Amos's questioning get to you. Just keep a cool head is all. Make out like you don't know what the hell he's talking about. That's all."

"Is he coming to see me?" Swenson asked. "Does he know who we are?"

"I don't know that," Carter said. "I'm just telling you that if he does come to see you, act like you don't know nothing. There's something else. Amos said that Slocum aims to kill us all."

"How would Amos know that?" said Swenson.

"He wouldn't tell me how he come by any of his information," Carter said. "I'm wondering if maybe Slocum hisself slipped in and had a talk with him."

"Slocum in town?" Swenson said.

"I'm guessing," said Carter. "Just remember what I said. That's all. I got to go see the others now. Just keep your head."

Carter led the way out of the room. The customer was gone. Swenson followed Carter to the front door and stepped out onto the sidewalk with him. From inside the marshal's office, Foss watched them through the front window. Carter started to walk away, but he stopped and shoved Swenson back inside, backing up in the doorway with him.

"Look," he said. "At Millicent's."

Swenson looked and saw Slocum going into Millicent's Eatery.

"He's here," Swenson said.

"Don't panic," said Carter.

"I don't mean to sit around and wait for him to come and kill me," said Swenson. He turned and went back into his store, back behind the counter, and came back out with a shotgun.

"What the hell are you doing with that?" Carter asked.

"I mean to get him first," said Swenson. "Get out of my way."

Carter grabbed Swenson by an arm, but Swenson jerked loose. "Leave me be," he said.

"Morley," said Carter, "he's a damn gunfighter."

"I got a scattergun here," Swenson said.

Carter started to say something more but stopped himself short. Yeah, he said to himself. Let him go. He'll kill Slocum or Slocum will kill him. Either way will be all right. Morley's too damn jumpy anyhow. He started walking back to his saloon. Just as he reached it, he saw Amos Foss come running from the marshal's office. He ducked on inside the Booze Palace to wait.

"Well, hello," Millicent said, as Slocum stepped inside. "I wasn't sure I'd ever see you again."

"I wasn't real sure myself," said Slocum, "but here I am. Can I get a cup of coffee?"

"Coming right up," she said.

Slocum found himself a table to his liking and sat down facing the door. Just then Swenson came barging in. Looking around quickly, he saw Slocum and raised the shotgun. Just in time, Slocum threw himself back, at the same time kicking over the table to make a shield. The blast of the shotgun filled the room and rattled the walls, and pellets spanged against the tabletop there in front of Slocum. Slocum stood up immediately after the shot. From behind the overturned table, he raised his Colt and fired. One shot thudded into the chest of Swenson.

Swenson gasped out loud, a sound of both surprise and horror. He looked down at his chest as he dropped the shotgun to the floor. He stood for a moment, weaving, then fell back through the door to land on the sidewalk outside. Foss came running up just in time to hear the shots and to see Swenson fall. He stopped and checked Swenson, finding him dead. Then he stepped over the body to go inside Millicent's. Slocum was just holstering his Colt.

"Slocum," Foss said, his voice threatening.

"I didn't have no choice," said Slocum. "Ask anyone here."

"I know you didn't," Foss said. "I saw him coming with

that gun. I tried to make it in time to stop him, but— well, I didn't make it."

Millicent ran over to Slocum's side. "Are you hurt?" she asked.

"Naw," he said. "I'm all right. I'm sorry this happened in here."

"But you are hurt," she said, taking hold of his left arm tenderly. He looked and saw that his arm was bleeding. Some of the bouncing pellets must have torn into it, but in the excitement, he hadn't felt anything.

"Better get Doc to take a look at that," Foss said.

"It ain't bad," Slocum said.

"Come with me," said Millicent. "I can take care of it." Then she raised her voice for her other customers to hear. "Whatever you're eating is on the house," she said. "Soon as you're done, I'm closing up for the day."

Slocum let her lead him to her back room, but just as they were going through the door, Foss spoke out to Slocum.

"I want you to leave town, Slocum," he said. "Get your arm patched up and ride on out. I don't care where you go, but I want you out of here."

"All I did was defend myself," Slocum said. "You can't run me out of town for that."

"I can if I figure you to be a danger to the community," said Foss. "I meant what I said. Get out of town."

Alone with Slocum inside her quarters and with the door locked, Millicent removed Slocum's shirt. She washed the wound, picked out some pellets and bound up the arm in clean white bandages. "That should do it," she said.

"Thank you," said Slocum. "It'll do fine."

"Can you tell me what's going on?" she asked.

He told her the whole story, including how his dalliance with her had kept him safely away from the camp the night that Harley had been killed.

"Oh, John," she said, "I'm so sorry."

"I never meant to imply that it was your fault," he said. "That's just the way it happened. That's all. There ain't no one to blame but Ace Carter and them that was with him, and I mean to get them all. There's three down now. Four to go."

"But Amos Foss just told you to get out of town," she said.

"I'll get," Slocum said, "but I won't go far."

"Let me fix you a meal first," she said. "You did come in here to eat, didn't you?"

"Well," he said, "that might have been on my mind as well."

She prepared him a steak with all the trimmings and he ate ravenously. Then he had a cup of coffee. She brought out the whiskey bottle and poured him a drink. When he was done with that, he said, "If I ain't out of here soon, ol' Foss is liable to come looking for me."

"Let him look," she said, and she put her arms around his shoulders. She leaned in to kiss his lips, and he responded by pulling her close to him and holding her tight. The kiss was long and lingering and wet. He started pulling at her dress and she pulled at the waistband of his trousers. Soon they were naked together, and she took his hand and led him to her bed. She crawled in and stretched out on her back, opening her thighs to invite him in. He was ready. He moved on top of her and let his weight down on her slowly and carefully, at the same time pressing his lips against hers.

She reached down with both hands to guide him inside her, and simultaneously they started to move. Their bodies were like a smooth machine with all parts working together in a beautiful rhythm. For a while it was slow and easy, but gradually the speed increased. Soon they were driving themselves against one another. He was driving himself harder and deeper inside her. Her moans of pleasure took on a desperate note. At last she squealed with delight, and then Slocum felt the release that he had been building toward. Soon they lay still, breathing deeply, spent, delighted with the wonders of their two bodies.

Slocum pulled out at last and rolled over onto his back. "Wait a minute," she said. She got up and left the room. In a moment she returned with a bowl of water and a towel. Lovingly, she washed him off, then dried him. Setting aside the bowl and towel, she leaned over him to give him a tender kiss.

"I hate to say it," she whispered, "but if I don't, you'll have to, and I'd rather say it than hear you say it."

"What's that?" he said.

"You'd better go," she said. "But John, be careful. You were lucky today. Watch out for yourself and stay safe."

Slocum walked over to his roan at the hitchrail and prepared to mount up. Amos Foss stepped out of his office. "Slocum," he asked, "where you going?"

"I'm leaving your town," said Slocum, "like you told me to do. Remember?"

"Where you going?" Foss asked.

"I don't think I need to tell you that," Slocum said. "You can tell me to get out of your town, but you can't tell me nothing after that. You are just a town marshal, ain't you?"

"That's right," Foss said.

"That there town limits sign on the road west," Slocum said. "Is it in the right legal spot?"

"It is," Foss said.

"When I'm beyond it then, you ain't got no say?" Slocum asked.

"That's right," Foss admitted. "But don't try to pull anything cute on me."

"Mr. Foss," said Slocum, "there ain't been nothing cute about me since I was a toddler—maybe not even then. I'll be seeing you around." He swung up onto the back of the roan, tipped his hat to Foss, and turned her to ride out of town.

"Slocum," Foss called out to him as he was riding away, "I know you mean to kill four more men. Men from my town. You'd better watch your ass."

Slocum waved and continued riding. He did not look back. Foss stormed angrily over to the Booze Palace and barged in. Almost immediately, he saw Ace Carter back at his favorite table and still drinking. Carter had a smug look on his face.

"You're under arrest, Carter," said Foss. "Come along with me."

"What the hell for?" Carter asked.

"Call it suspicion for right now," said Foss. "Come on."

"Suspicion of what?" asked Carter.

"If I knew it wouldn't be suspicion, now, would it?" Foss said. "Take out any weapons you have on you and lay them on the table. Do it now."

Foss was so angry that Carter decided he had better do as he was told. He pulled out a pocket pistol and placed it on the table. "That's all I got," he said.

"It had better be," said Foss. "Now come along."

He started walking with Carter toward the jail, hurrying him along.

"You won't be able to keep me in there," Carter said. "You got nothing on me."

"I'll keep you as long as I can," said Foss.

"I'll see that you lose your job for this, too," said Carter. "This ain't no way to treat one of the leading citizens of this here town. I got influence, and you know it. I'll be out of jail, and you'll be out of a job."

"Shut up," Foss said. "There's four men dead because of you. You know it, and I know it. Maybe I can't prove it just yet, but if Slocum doesn't kill all of you first, I'll get to the bottom of it. You can count on that."

They reached the jail and went inside. Foss shoved Carter into a cell, shut the door, and locked it. Carter took a bar in each hand and shook the door. Then he let go of the bars, turned away, and paced to the window at the far wall. Stopping, he turned to face Foss who had already taken a seat behind his desk.

"You son of a bitch," Carter said, "the least you could a done was let me bring my goddamn bottle along with me."

Foss jerked open a desk drawer and pulled out a bottle. He stood up and walked over to the cell. Handing the bottle through the bars, he said, "Go on. Get drunk as hell for all I care." Then he went back to his chair. Carter uncorked the bottle and took a long drink. "Maybe if you get drunk enough," Foss said, "you'll tell me what I want to know."

"Is that what you think?" Carter asked. "You think if you keep me in here you'll scare some kind of confession out of me? Well, forget it, asshole. I ain't got nothing to confess. I don't know nothing about all that shit."

"And I reckon Morley Swenson going after Slocum with a shotgun right after you paid him a visit was just a coincidence, huh?" Foss said. "I reckon you don't know anything about that either."

"I don't know why the dumb shit did that," said Carter.

"Maybe not," Foss said, "but maybe those other three might start getting nervous with three already dead and you locked up in here. Maybe one of them will slip up and tell me something. We'll see."

Carter didn't answer. He hadn't thought of that. What would Hedley do, or Barber, or Cain, when they heard that he had been arrested and thrown in jail? Sure, Foss was right. With Trumbull, Chapman, and Swenson all dead, they would be getting nervous. That could be a real problem.

7

Slocum rode out to Harley Duggan's grave. This time he found it undisturbed. He dismounted, took off his hat, and stood at the graveside for a moment in silence. Finally he said, "Harley, old pard, I got four of them. There's three left, and I'll get them too. Only thing is, I got me a little problem with the marshal, and I need to let it rest a few days. Thought I'd let you know." He paused a moment, and then he said, "You remember that little lady in the eating place that you was interested in and I sent you out of town? Well, me and her has got real well acquainted. That was a dirty trick I played on you. Anyhow, to sort of make up for it, there's another one out yonder a ways, all alone on a little ranch. Anyhow, I think she's all alone. I mean to ride out there and find out, and if she is, and if I can get to her, this one'll be for you, pardner. It'll help me pass a few days, and then I'll get back after them four. I'll be having a good time, and they'll be stewing, wondering what happened to me. Well, so long, Harley."

Halley Lawson stood on her porch, rifle in hand, watching the rider approach. She waited until she recognized the roan and then the rider, and she put the rifle aside. A smile spread across her face. When he came even closer, she yelled out a welcome.

"Slocum!" she shouted. "Ride on in."

He rode to the corral, unsaddled the roan, and turned it in with the other horses. His big Appaloosa snorted and ran to the fence to nuzzle in his hands. He talked to it for a few minutes, gave it a final pat and a promise to return soon. Then he walked over to the porch. "Howdy, ma'am," he said.

"I kind of thought I'd be seeing you again," Halley said.

"I got to ask you," he said, "is there a Mister Lawson?"

"Hell no," she said. "I wouldn't have one. The last one that come out here and asked me was a no-good loafing bum. He wanted my ranch, but he wanted me to do all the work. I run his ass off right quick."

Slocum grinned.

"Well," he said, scratching his head under his hat, "I don't want your ranch, and I ain't the marrying kind. I would like to hang out around here a few days though. I'd work to pay for you putting up with me."

"Come on in the house," she said. She picked up her rifle, turned, and walked inside. Slocum followed her and shut the door behind himself. As he turned toward the room, Halley flung herself at him, throwing both arms around his neck. The force of her body threw him back against the door, and he looked down into her face with a surprised expression. "I know why you come back," she said, "and it weren't to do no ranch work." She pulled his head down to meet hers and pressed wet lips against his mouth. Her tongue snaked out and writhed its way inside his mouth, creeping around and exploring.

He reached around her and put a hand on each of her ass cheeks, pulling her up and against him. Finally, he moved his hands to her shoulders and pushed her away. "Let me take off my hat at least," he said. She started pulling at her own clothes.

"Take off your hat and ever'thing else," she said.

Leaving a trail of clothes across the room, she jumped onto her bed. Slocum followed her example. When he moved to the bed, ready for her, she grabbed him again and threw him down on his back. In a flash she had mounted him and was riding him hard. "Wahoo!" she shouted. Just when he felt like a bronc that was almost bucked out, she stopped and got off. She got on all fours there beside him, and she said, "Get behind me, cowboy." He got up on his knees and moved behind her. He drove into her from there, and as he plunged in and out, she wriggled her delighted ass hard against his pelvis.

"Ride 'em, cowboy," she whooped.

Slocum decided that he'd had about enough of this. He backed off, grabbed her and flipped her over on her back. Then he threw himself on top of her and drove himself into her over and over again, hard and fast. At last he exploded, shooting great spurts deep into her anxious tunnel. Finished and nearly exhausted, he rolled over onto his back.

"I really will help with the work around here," he said. "For a few days."

Not bothering to get dressed, she got up and fixed them a meal. They ate naked, and they washed the meal down with several cups of coffee. In spite of the way in which she had ambushed him, Slocum thought that Halley Lawson was a remarkable woman. There was no foolishness about her. She was a hardheaded, hardworking woman running a small ranch alone. She was a businesswoman, and when it came to getting her way, she was all business. Slocum had just found that out. He liked her, but he made up his mind that she would not take charge of him again like that.

"Well, lady," he said, finishing off his last cup of coffee, "shall we get to work? What needs doing around here that I can help with?"

He picked up his trousers and started to pull them on. She hurried over to his side and laid a hand on his shoulder. "Ain't nothing that can't wait till tomorrow," she said. "Right now, we're here nekkid and alone. We can play around some more. Maybe the whole day and night. In the morning'll be soon enough to get back to work."

He hesitated and gave her a look.

"That'd be all right," she said. Then her whole tone

changed, and she gave him a pleading look. "Wouldn't it?"

He smiled down at her and dropped his jeans back to the floor. "It's your ranch," he said. "If you say the morning's soon enough, then I reckon the work'll wait."

Slocum confided the whole story of the murder of Harley Duggan to Halley. He also told her of his intention to avenge Harley's death. He told her what had transpired already, including his having been run out of Whizbang by the town marshal. He told her finally that he had allowed himself to be run out of town for one reason: to let Ace Carter and the others stew for a few days, worrying about when he might show up again. He figured, he told her, that her place might be a good place to hang out those few days. He also meant to pick up his Appaloosa. Everything was out in the open now. There was no longer any reason to sneak around.

The next morning Slocum split firewood, and when that was done, he went to work mending the corral fence. He noted that Halley was doing a pretty good job with this place, but he also noted that it was too much work for a woman alone. Some things had gotten pretty run down. He figured that he could take care of those things in the few days he had given himself. It was a pretty damn good bargain all the way around.

"Amos, you son of a bitch," Ace Carter shouted, "how goddamn long do you think you can make me set in this here jail cell?"

"Long as I figure it's necessary, I reckon," Foss answered. "There's an investigation underway, and you're a material witness."

"I want to see a goddamn lawyer," said Carter.

"Ace," said Foss, "you know damn well there ain't no lawyers in Whizbang. That's one of the things I like about our little town. No lawyers."

"But there's laws," Carter protested. "You can't just go around throwing citizens in jail like this. You got to have charges. You got to have evidence. You got to go find me a lawyer."

"That's not my job," Foss said. "The court appoints lawyers for them that can't afford them. I ain't the court, and you can afford to pay your own lawyer, anyhow. If you got any real friends in this town, maybe one of them can go out and hunt you up a lawyer. But even if you were to get you a lawyer, he'd have to go to the judge, and you know as well as I do that the judge ain't scheduled to come into Whizbang for another three weeks."

"This ain't fair," said Carter, "and it ain't legal."

"You get me a court order saying that," Foss said, "and I'll turn you loose. As far as what's legal is concerned, it ain't legal for a group of citizens to form a lynch mob and to try to choke information out of someone. It sure ain't legal for them to commit a murder under the pretense of upholding the law."

"You got no proof that I had a damn thing to do with that," Carter said.

"I got pretty damn good circumstantial evidence," Foss said, "and many a man has been hanged on circumstantial evidence."

"Damn you," Carter said.

"Ace," said Foss, "if a lawyer should happen to come in here, I'll tell him you'd like to talk with him."

Chunk Hedley, Doby Barber, and Sammy Cain sat together in the Booze Palace. They were sharing a bottle of whiskey at a table in a far corner of the room, safely out of earshot of anyone else in the place. Even so, when they spoke, they spoke in low voices, and they leaned across the table toward one another like the conspirators they were.

"Amos run Slocum out of town," Barber said. "We're safe now."

"But Amos also throwed Ace in jail," said Hedley. "What the hell do you think that means?"

"What that means," said Sammy Cain, "is that Amos don't want no one shooting up his town. That's why he run Slocum off. What it also means is that Amos wants to pin the killing of Slocum's partner on us. That's why he stuck Ace in jail. He don't want Slocum gunning us down. He wants to see us hang legal and proper."

"Well, what the hell are we going to do?" Hedley asked. "If it comes to a hanging, do you really think Ace will hang by hisself? Hell, no. He'll tell on us, all right. He'll take us along with him. He ain't so tough as he lets on. Remember how he acted whenever Slocum just only nicked his shoulder? He'll talk. He'll talk all right. He'll put all our necks in a noose. That's what the chickenshit son of a bitch'll do."

"Way I understand it," Barber said, "there ain't been no charges filed against Ace yet. Amos is just suspicious is all. He's trying to scare Ace into talking. Hell, if there's no charges filed, there won't be no trial, and if that don't happen, there ain't no reason for Ace to get scared and spill his guts out."

"That's right," Hedley agreed. "And Amos don't know that we was with Ace that night. Hell, no one really knows."

"Dutch knows," said Cain. "He seen us all leave here together. And Slocum knows. He got a good look at all of us."

The other two looked at one another with big round eyes that shifted back and forth.

"Well, Slocum's gone," said Hedley.

"He'll be back," said Cain, "and we got to be ready for it when he comes."

Just then Amos Foss walked into the saloon, and the three conspirators all felt as if Foss had given them a special hard look. "He knows," said Barber. "He's looking at us right now. He knows."

"Bullshit," said Hedley. "How could he know anything?"

"He'd know if Ace told him," Barber said. "Ace has been talking. That's how he knows."

"Shut up," said Cain. "Maybe he knows and maybe he don't. Maybe Ace has been talking and maybe he ain't.

But it won't make no difference unless he talks in court. One thing's for sure though."

"What's that?" Hedley asked.

"We got to make sure Ace don't talk," Cain said. "You two make sure Amos hangs around here for a while."

He shoved back his chair and stood up.

"Where you going?" Barber asked nervously.

"I got something to do," said Cain. "Just keep Amos busy. That's all. You hear?"

Cain headed out the back door of the Booze Palace. Barber and Hedley watched nervously as he left. They looked at one another and then over at Amos Foss. Barber tossed down a jigger of whiskey. "Well, what the hell is Sammy up to?" he asked.

"How the hell should I know?" Hedley said. He was staring at Foss, who had stopped at the bar and ordered a drink. "Hell, I don't even want to know. Just keep on watching Amos, that's all."

"What are we supposed to do if he starts to leave?" Barber asked. "How are we supposed to keep him in here anyway?"

"Aw, hell," said Hedley. "Just watch me."

He stood up and casually walked over to the bar to stand beside Foss. Dutch asked him what he wanted, and he ordered a shot. "Can I buy you one, Amos?" he asked.

"No, thanks, Chunk," Foss said. "I just got one, and that's all I need for a spell."

"Say, Amos," Hedley said, "there's something I been meaning to ask you."

Foss waited a bit, and when Hedley didn't say anything more, he said, "Well, what is it?"

"I heard you got old Ace locked up in the jailhouse," Hedley said.

"That ain't a question," said Foss.

"Well, is it true?" asked Hedley. "You got Ace locked up?"

"That's right," Foss said.

"Well, how come?" Hedley asked. "What'd Ace do?"

"Right now," Foss said, "that's between me and Ace."

"Huh," said Hedley. "That's real curious now. I sure can't imagine old Ace doing anything to get hisself locked up for. He's a real public-spirited fella, old Ace is. Upstanding citizen and all. You know what I mean?"

"I get your drift, Chunk," Foss said. He finished his drink and turned to leave. Hedley put a hand on his arm.

"Hold up a minute, Amos," he said. "Me and Doby was talking back there in the corner about something. Come on back and join us for a bit, would you?"

"What's it about?" Foss said.

"I'd rather not talk about it up here where everyone can hear," Hedley said. "Come on. It won't take long."

Foss followed Hedley back to the corner table where Barber waited nervously. As Hedley took a chair and offered one to Foss, Barber gave the marshal a nervous greeting. "Now what's this all about?" Foss asked.

"We been talking about them killings around here," Hedley said. "Some says it's that drifter that come through here that's been doing them. Well, I guess we all know it was him that killed poor old Morley. But we was wondering what you know about Gary and Chilly. You reckon that Slocum fella done them in, too?"

"I'll tell you what I think," Foss said. "I think you two know a hell of a lot more about this whole mess than I do."

Sammy Cain found the door to the marshal's office unlocked. He looked up and down the street to make sure no one was watching, and then he let himself in. He shut the door behind himself, stood a moment looking around, and then he walked over to the cell door. Ace Carter saw him and jumped up from the cot where he had been stretched out.

"Sammy," he said, "it's about time you come. You got to get me out of here. Ride over to Springtown and get me a lawyer. Get him to draw up some kind of paper to make Amos let me out of here. The son of a bitch ain't even charged me with nothing but just only suspicion. That's all he said. Suspicion. I said suspicion of what, and he said if he knowed he wouldn't be just suspicious. He can't do me that way. You ride over to Springtown and get me that legal paper. Get going now."

"I don't know, Ace," Cain said. "That's a long ride over there for nothing."

"What do you mean for nothing?" said Carter gripping the bars and pressing his face into them. "Get Doby over here. He'll make that ride for me. Go get Doby."

"If Amos ain't charged you with nothing," Cain said, "then why's he keeping you in here?"

"What?" Carter said.

"Why has Amos got you locked up?" Cain asked again.

"Hell, how should I know?" said Carter.

"Is he trying to get you to tell about what happened out yonder to that cowboy?" Cain asked. "Is he maybe trying to sweat it out of you?"

"I—I don't know," said Carter. "Who cares? Just get me out of here. Hell, if you don't want to ride over to Springtown, just get the keys right now and let me out. We'll deal with Amos later. Get the keys. They're right over there."

Carter stretched an arm through the bars to point at a ring of keys on a peg on the wall just behind Foss's big office chair.

"Maybe you've done told him something," Cain said.

"What?" said Carter.

"I've heard tell," said Cain, "that sometimes when the law gets its hands on one man, if that one man tells on others, then he gets off easy. I heard tell about that. Is that what you done to us, Ace?"

As he was saying those last words, Cain slipped his revolver out of its holster and pointed its muzzle at Ace Carter's chest. Carter backed away from the cell door, holding his hands out in front of himself. A look of horror and disbelief came over his face.

"No, Sammy," he said. "I ain't said a thing. Sammy. Don't shoot. Just let me out of here, and we'll take care of this mess together. Sammy. Don't do it!"

His last few words were screamed out, but even so, they

were drowned out by the roar of two shots from Sammy Cain's revolver. Carter grabbed at his chest, staggered back, and fell against the far cell wall. His eyes wide and staring at Cain, his legs losing their strength, he slid slowly down the wall to come to rest in a sitting position. A long smear of blood on the wall trailed him down. He sat still. To make doubly sure, Sammy Cain fired one more shot into the body. Then looking quickly around, he ran for the back door and left the marshal's office.

8

As Sammy Cain slipped back into the Booze Palace through the back door, Amos Foss, having heard the shots, was running out the front door. Cain hurried over to the table where Hedley and Barber still sat. "Come on," he said. Others in the saloon, curious, ran after Foss, and the three conspirators joined them.

Foss ran out into the middle of the street and looked around. A man down near the marshal's office saw him and shouted, "Shots come from the jail, Amos!" Foss ran to the building that was both his office and the jail, and the crowd ran after him. Reaching the building, he stopped in the doorway, gun in hand. He turned to face the crowd. "Stay back," he yelled. Then he went inside. He looked around quickly to make sure the shooter was no longer in there, and then he saw Ace Carter sitting on the cell floor, his back against the wall, his chin on his chest. Carter's chest was covered in blood, and a smear of blood ran down the wall behind him. He didn't need to check closer. He could tell right away that Carter was dead.

"Damn," he said. He walked back to the door and stepped out to face the crowd. "Someone's killed Ace Carter," he said.

"What?" someone shouted.

"Who was it?" another asked.

"It was that Slocum," shouted Sammy Cain.

Someone said, "I thought he'd left town."

"He sneaked back in to kill Ace," Barber said, having picked up on Cain's scheme.

"We better get a posse after him!" Hedley yelled out, and many voices joined his. It took Foss a while to settle the crowd.

"Did anyone see Slocum come into town?" he asked.

No one had.

"We don't know yet who it was that did this," he said. "Now all of you just go on about your business, and leave me to take care of my job. Go on now. Go home, or go back to work. Go on."

Slowly the crowd dispersed, mumbling all the while. Cain put a hand on Barber's shoulder and glanced at Hedley. "Let's go finish our drinks," he said. "Everything's taken care of now."

Back in the Booze Palace at their same table in the far corner, Barber leaned over close in to Cain. "Was that you done that?" he asked.

"Why, I don't know what you're talking about," Cain said. "It sure as hell looks like that Slocum sneaked on back in here and got ol' Ace, though, don't it?"

"Well, yeah," Barber said. "I guess it does. I guess it does at that." He laughed a nervous laugh. Then Cain's face took on a deadly serious expression, and Cain reached over and took hold of Barber's shirt, pulling him close. Cain spoke through clenched teeth.

"What you don't know won't hurt you," he said, "and what you don't know won't hurt me. You got that?"

"Yeah," Barber said. "Yeah. I got it. It sure as hell looks like that Slocum done it. That's what it looks like to me."

"Sammy," said Hedley, "what do reckon that Slocum is really up to?"

Slocum and Halley were riding her west range. Slocum rode his big Appaloosa, and it felt good to him to have the stallion between his legs again. Halley rode the roan mare that Slocum had bought from her. They heard a cow bawling, and the sound seemed to come from over a small hill to their right. "Let's check it out," Halley said, and without waiting for a response from Slocum, she turned the roan and headed over the hill. Slocum followed.

As they topped the rise they could see the cow bogged down in a muddy pond. Slocum snaked out a rope and threw a loop over the cow's head. Wrapping the other end of the rope around his saddlehorn, he backed the Appaloosa out, pulling the rope taut. The cow bawled and strained but did not budge.

"It ain't working," Halley said.

Slocum loosened the rope from his saddlehorn and handed it to Halley.

"You take it," he said.

"What are you going to do?" she said.

"Just take the rope," he said.

She took it and looped the end around her own saddlehorn as Slocum dismounted. He sat down on the ground and pulled off his boots. Then he stood up and peeled off his clothes. Walking gingerly on his bare feet, he waded into the bog. The deep mud sucked at his feet and pulled him down. He was knee deep in mud, and it took all his strength to move his feet forward. Reaching the side of the bawling cow, he could feel the mud pulling around his thighs. He reached under the murky water to get his arms underneath the cow's belly, and as Halley backed the roan, he lifted and strained all his muscles.

Finally, the cow lurched forward. The suddenness of her movement threw Slocum off balance, and only the mud sucking at his legs kept him from falling over. Free at last, the cow lumbered up onto dry land, then stood panting from the strain and exhaustion. Halley dismounted and took the loop off the cow's head. "Good job!" she shouted happily.

"Only one thing," Slocum said.

"What's that?" she asked.

"Now I'm stuck," he said.

Halley threw Slocum the loop, and he pulled it over his head and shoulders, fitting it under his arms. She climbed back on the roan and started backing up. Slocum came free with a loud sucking sound and found himself dragged out on the dry ground. "Whoa!" he shouted. "Stop her. Don't drag me."

Halley stopped the horse, and Slocum got up to his feet. He took the rope off and stood there looking helpless. Halley started to laugh.

"What's so damn funny?" he said.

"You oughta see yourself," she said. "You look like you're made out of mud. You look like a nekkid mud man."

"Very funny," he said. "Now how am I going to get all this shit offa me?"

"I'll get your clothes," she said. "I guess you'll just have to ride back to the house nekkid—if your horse'll let you on him."

Amos Foss sat in his office alone. The body of Ace Carter had been taken away, but the problem of his murder was still with Foss. He wondered if Slocum had somehow managed to slip back into town unseen and do the deed, then get out clean. It was no secret: Slocum had sworn to kill Carter and the others. Three others. Foss was suspicious of Cain, Barber, and Hedley, but he really had no proof. He knew that Slocum knew who the three were, but Slocum had not given him any names.

Foss knew that Carter had been the leader of the mob, but he did not know who the rest of the mob had been. He only knew that Trumbull, Chapman, and Swenson had been among them. He only knew the dead ones. He was afraid that he would not know the identities of the remaining three for sure until they, too, were dead. Then he wondered, would it really matter? What the seven men had done to Slocum's partner had been terrible. They deserved their fate, and Slocum deserved to be the one to deliver it.

He had even admitted to Slocum that in his place, he would likely be doing the same thing. But Foss was a lawman. He was supposed to stop killing. He was supposed to make the law do the job and to keep revenge and the lust for justice out of the hands of ordinary citizens. But then, he thought, this Slocum is not an ordinary citizen.

Slocum had said that he was no murderer. Foss knew that Swenson had made the first move against Slocum, and Slocum had said that the other two had done the same. Slocum would force them into a showdown and kill them happily, but would he commit a cold-blooded murder? Foss could not be sure. He wondered. But then, he thought, he really did not think so. He did not believe that Slocum had killed Carter. It just didn't seem like Slocum's style.

Foss considered arresting Cain or Barber or Hedley, but he already tried that tactic with Carter, and it had gotten him nowhere. It had only gotten Carter murdered. Likely Carter had it coming to him, but still, Foss didn't like having been accessory to the crime, however unknowing or unwilling. He felt like he had to do something, but he could think of nothing to do other than to try to keep an eye on the three suspects and to watch out for the return of Slocum.

Slocum saddled the Appaloosa and bundled up his few belongings. Halley walked over to the corral to join him there. "You leaving?" she asked him.

"It's time I got back to business," he said.

"Well," she said, "I ain't going to try to hold you, but it's been fun, and you've been a big help while you was here. What about your roan?"

"She's yours," Slocum said.

"Then I owe you some money," she said.

"No," he said. "You don't owe me anything. I needed a place to lay low for a spell, and you gave it to me. Let's call it even."

"Okay," she said, "but anytime you need a place to hole up, you're welcome here."

"Thanks, Halley," he said. "I'll remember that."

He swung into the saddle, tipped his hat to her, then

turned and rode off without looking back. Halley stood and watched him go for a while. Then she turned back to her work. Yeah, she thought, it was fun while it lasted.

Slocum's thoughts were back on the business he had promised to take care of. There were four more men to kill. He knew their names, and he knew their faces. He knew Ace Carter to be the leader of the gang. The other three were Hedley, Barber, and Cain. He knew the three faces and the three names, but he didn't know which name belonged to which face. It didn't matter. He would get them. He would get all four of them. Then his promise would be fulfilled.

It was a two-day ride back to Whizbang, and Slocum had spent several days with Halley. He figured that he'd been gone long enough to have the four men he was after off their guard. He had left Whizbang on orders from the town marshal. His prey had probably decided, because of his long absence, that Amos Foss had scared him off for good. He'd catch them by surprise.

Of course, Foss could be a problem. He had ordered Slocum out of town, and if Slocum were to ride back in town, Foss might actually try to arrest him. Slocum didn't relish the thought of having to shoot it out with Foss, but he didn't intend to let the marshal throw him in jail either. He had no intention of letting Foss or anyone else stop him from avenging Harley's murder. All the long slow day of riding, he mulled these things over. Then he made a camp for the night.

It was a lonely camp. He thought of the times he had camped with Harley, and he recalled the conversations they'd had together, the good-natured banter back and forth, the joking insults and teasing. He missed Harley, and he wondered if he would ever again find a partner he could ride with, someone he could spend as much time with as he had with Harley. He doubted it. Well, he'd spent most of his life traveling alone. He could do it again.

The second day of travel seemed longer than the first. Slocum stopped only once, somewhere around noon, to fix himself a meal. He rode into the evening and was relieved when the sun dropped low in the sky and the air cooled off a bit. When at last he found himself looking down on Whizbang, he rode almost to the sign that marked the limits of the town, the limits of Amos Foss's jurisdiction. He dismounted and built his camp.

It wasn't long into the next morning before the word had gotten around Whizbang about the camp just outside of town. Slocum was sitting on the ground cross-legged, sipping coffee beside his fire. He looked up to see Amos Foss riding in his direction. Casually, he slipped the Colt out of its holster and laid it beside himself. Foss rode on up and stopped. He looked over the little camp with its makeshift tent, bedroll, and fire.

"Howdy, Slocum," he said.

"Howdy, Marshal," said Slocum. "Come on down and have a cup of coffee."

"All right," said Foss, and he dismounted. He walked over and sat across the fire from Slocum. Slocum poured another cup full of coffee and handed it to Foss. "I figured you'd be back," Foss said.

"You figured right," said Slocum.

"I told you to stay away," Foss said. "I told you to let the law handle this situation."

"That was while we were in town," Slocum said. "We ain't in your town just now. I checked on that with you. Remember?"

"I remember," Foss said. "But you ain't far enough outside of my jurisdiction to suit me."

"That's tough," Slocum said. "You ain't planning to shoot it out with me, are you? You being such an upholder of law and order and such."

"No," Foss said, "I guess not. I thought about it. Tell me, Slocum, have you been back to town since I ran you out?"

"I haven't been close to your town since then. Not till I set up this camp last night," Slocum said. "Why do you ask?"

"Someone killed Ace Carter," Foss said. "Murdered him in cold blood. He was unarmed and locked up in my jail cell."

"Damn," said Slocum. "Goddamn it. I wanted him. I wanted him more than all the others. The son of a bitch was the ring leader."

"There's some in town saying that you done it," Foss said. "They say you swore to kill him and the others, and that you slipped into town and killed him."

"If I'd a done it," Slocum said, "I wouldn't a slipped in to do it. And he'd have had a gun on him. I don't do murders."

"You told me that before," said Foss. He sipped some coffee. It had cooled a bit. Slocum finished his own cup and poured himself some more.

"So Carter's dead, huh?" he said. "You wouldn't just be saying that to throw me off the track, would you?"

"He's dead all right," said Foss.

"That just leaves three," Slocum said.

"What are their names?" Foss asked. Slocum didn't answer.

"Barber, Hedley, Cain?" Foss asked.

"What if they are?" Slocum asked.

"I can arrest them and charge them and hold them for trial," said Foss.

"What good would that do?" Slocum said. "There's no real proof. They'd just get off."

"All we can do is try," said the marshal.

"I can do more than that," Slocum said, "and I mean to."

"If you come into town—"

"I ain't moving from right here," said Slocum. "You tell them that. If they don't like it, they can come out here and try to do something about it. I'll be right here waiting for them."

"That's what you want, isn't it?" Foss said. "You figure if you sit here long enough, just you being here will eat away at them till they can't take it no more. Then they'll come out to get you. They'll come shooting, and you can kill them in self-defense."

"Sounds good to me," Slocum said. "More coffee?"

Hedley, Barber, and Cain stood in the middle of the street looking out toward Slocum's camp. Foss had come back into town some hours earlier, and Slocum still sat alone beside his fire. Even from their distance away, they could see that he was smoking a cigar.

"Look at the son of a bitch just a setting there," Hedley said. "What the hell's he think he's doing anyhow?"

"He's waiting for us," said Cain.

"Waiting for us?" Barber said.

"Yeah," said Cain. "If we go up there gunning for him, he won't face no murder charges."

"Well, I ain't going out there," said Barber. "He can set there and rot in the sun. I ain't going."

"How many days you think you can go on watching him set there like that?" Cain asked. "You think you can take it for a week? Longer?"

"He'll get tired of it after a few days, won't he?" Hedley said. "Hell, he'll run out of food and water. He'll have to leave."

"If he has to leave," Cain said, "he'll come back."

"Well, what are we going to do?" Barber asked.

"Nothing," said Cain. "For now."

It was a dark night, and the campfire burned low. Slocum slept a distance away from it, so that anyone trying to slip up on him in the night wouldn't easily find him. He was a light sleeper, and the chances were that he'd hear them and see them before they saw him. He had just stretched out for the night when he heard approaching footsteps. He picked up his Colt and waited and watched. Soon a dark figure loomed up near the fire. As he saw the figure in the dim firelight, he heard the soft voice.

"John?"

It was Millicent. He stood up and walked toward her. "I'm over here," he said. "What are you doing out here?"

"Everyone in town knows you're out here," she said,

"and everyone's talking about why you're camped out here, too. It's to stay out of Amos Foss's jurisdiction. Isn't that right?"

"He did tell me to stay out of town," Slocum admitted. "But you didn't answer my question."

She held out a covered basket she had carried along with her. "I thought you might like a home-cooked meal," she said.

9

The food was wonderful, but he had more than just a good meal that night. When he was through eating, they didn't even bother going into the tent. Millicent just hiked up her skirt and rode Slocum right there on his bedroll. It was a distance away from the fire, so no one could see them there after dark. No one came by anyhow, so there were no problems. After she was well satisfied, and he was well spent, they lay together quietly for a while before they started talking. Then they talked about Whizbang.

"I don't really like it," she said. "I'm just kind of stuck here. I don't make enough money to pack up and get out. I'm just barely hanging on."

"This country's rough on a woman alone," Slocum said. "You ought to find yourself another man. One that would make you a good living."

"Like those solid citizens in Whizbang?" she said. "No thanks."

"Yeah," he said. "I know what you mean. I've already seen enough of them solid citizens to last me a long time."

"Why don't you just ride on out, John?" she said. "Four of them are dead. Isn't that enough?"

"There's three alive," he said. "I can't rest till I get them, too. I made a promise."

"You could get yourself killed keeping that promise,"

she said. "I wouldn't want to see that happen."

"I'm glad you care," he said, "but don't worry about me. I can take care of myself all right. I'm more worried about you being stuck here in this damn town."

"Oh, I'll manage," she said. "It would be nice to get out, though, maybe have a little place out somewhere, a farm or a ranch. Oh, well." She stood up and straightened her clothes a bit. "I'd better get back while it's still dark," she said. "I don't want anyone seeing me come down from here in the morning. Besides, I need to get ready for my breakfast crowd."

"Likely some saw you come up here last night," Slocum said. "How you going to handle that?"

"I'll just tell them that your money is like anyone else's," she said. "I'll tell them that I sold you a supper."

Millicent had a busy morning at the Eatery, but when the rush was over, and things began to slow down, Amos Foss came in. He sat at a table by himself, and when Millicent came over, he ordered coffee and some breakfast. By the time she had served him, he was the only customer left in her place. When he had finished his meal, and she had cleared away his dishes, she came back to the table to refill his coffee cup. He thanked her and asked her to sit down. She did.

"I saw you go out to Slocum's camp last night," he said.

She sat and looked at him for a moment. When he didn't say anymore, she said, "Am I supposed to say something to that? It wasn't a question."

"I guess I want to ask you what you were up to," he said. "Why you went up there. What were you doing? I guess I want to ask those questions, but I guess that it's really none of my business."

Millicent flushed slightly. "I don't really think that it's any of your business," she said, "but if you really saw me, you should have seen that I was carrying a covered basket. I took him a hot meal. That's my business, you know. It's how I make my living."

"I see," Foss said, but she could tell that he wasn't really satisfied with her answer.

"Did you keep watching to see how long I was up there, Amos?" she said.

"No, Millicent," he said. "I didn't do that. I wouldn't spy on you. Like you said, it's not my business. I wouldn't have mentioned it at all except that—well, as long as Slocum's around, there's going to be trouble."

"What's that got to do with me taking a meal out to him?" she asked.

"Probably nothing at all," he said. "Maybe he said something to you that he wouldn't tell me. Maybe you learned something that might help me out with this problem. I don't know. I'm sorry I brought it up."

He started to get up, but she stopped him. "Wait a minute," she said. "Maybe I was too defensive. I understand what you're up against, but I understand too what Slocum's feeling—why he feels like he has to do what he's doing. I didn't learn anything that would help you, Amos. All I know is that he means to kill those men. And that he's as upset about Carter as you are—for different reasons, of course."

"Thanks, Millicent," Foss said.

"Amos," she said, "if I did know something, I don't know if I'd tell you."

"I understand that, too," he said. "Are you in love with Slocum?"

She sat still looking thoughtful for a long moment. Then, "No," she said. "I don't think so. I like him. I like him very much. He's fascinating in a way. He's comfortable. But he's a drifter, Amos. He'll be on his way when this is all over. He's sure not the kind of man a woman ought to go falling for."

"I maybe shouldn't have asked that question," Foss said. "It wasn't an official question. It was more, well, personal. I—"

"You want some more coffee, Amos?" she said, interrupting him on purpose. She wasn't at all sure that she wanted to hear the rest of what he was about to say.

• • •

Sammy Cain stood in the middle of the street looking up toward Slocum's camp. From the sidewalk, Hedley saw him. He walked out to join him. Hedley too looked toward Slocum. "He's still out there," he said. "The son of a bitch." His voice was quavering.

"Course he is," said Cain. "He ain't leaving. He ain't about to. He's waiting for us to go up there to him."

"Well, I sure ain't going," said Hedley.

"None of us are," said Cain. "That would be damn stupid."

"I ain't stupid," said Hedley.

"We got to do something, though," Cain said. "We got to do something. Chunk, I want you to round up some of the boys for a meeting. Get Gordon and Murf and ol' Alf. Tell them to meet with us at the saloon. We'll use the back room. Oh yeah. Be sure and tell Doby to be there, too."

"You ain't going to tell them—"

"Shut up, Chunk," Cain said. "I ain't going to tell them nothing. I don't want you to tell them nothing either 'cept that I want to meet with them. That's all. You got it? Tell them it's important though."

"Yeah," Hedley said.

"Get going then," said Cain. "And tell them right now. Hurry it up. I'll be over there in the back room waiting."

Slocum saw the two men in the street, saw them looking in his direction. He recognized them as two of the three he was after. He wondered what they were thinking, what they were planning. He wondered how long they would put up with his sitting there watching their town. Sooner or later, he knew, they would do something. One at a time or all three at once, they would come after him. That was the moment he was waiting for. That would be when he would get them. He didn't even consider the other possibility—that they would get him.

He cleaned his Colt and his Winchester methodically. He put them back together and reloaded them. Then he heated some beans and made some coffee. He ate, then sat back to enjoy coffee and a good cigar, and to continue to watch the town below. He saw Amos Foss come out of Millicent's Eatery and wondered whether or not the lawman had quizzed her up regarding her actions the night before. He saw the two men who had been watching him go their separate ways.

Sammy Cain walked into the Booze Palace. He did not even slow down as he walked through the main room, past Dutch at his place behind the bar. "I'm going to the back room," he said curtly. "Bring a bottle and six glasses." Cain went on into the back room to wait for the others. Dutch prepared the order and carried it to him on a tray. He set the tray down on the long table there. Then he went back to his station. Soon he saw Doby Barber come in and go directly to the back room. In another minute or so, Gordon Slick did the same. Dutch continued to watch as Murf Richie, Alf Badger, and finally Chunk Hedley all went into the room. When Hedley went in, he shut the door. It was quiet in the room until Hedley took a seat. Cain poured a drink and shoved it over to him. The other five already had drinks in front of them.

"Well, Sammy," said Gordon Slick, "what's this all about?"

"Yeah," said Murf Richie. "I don't mind drinking your whiskey, but I don't believe that you called us all over here just to buy us a drink."

A chuckle went around the room, and Cain interrupted it.

"I called y'all together here cause we got ourselves a serious problem here in our little town," he said. "We got a problem that our own town marshal Amos Foss ain't willing to take care of. Y'all likely heard that an out-of-work cowboy got hisself killed outside of town not too long ago. We don't know what happened to him—don't know nothing about that, but his partner, name of Slocum, got it in his head that this here town is to blame for whatever it was that happened out there. He's done killed four citizens of this town, four upstanding citizens, all friends of mine and friends of yours. There was Chilly Trumbull, Gary Chapman, Morley Swenson, and Ace Carter. All dead. All murdered by Slocum.

"Now, Amos is so damn confused over the whole goddamn thing that he actually had old Ace locked up in jail. Think about that. Just think about it. Old Ace Carter locked up in a jail cell, our jail. And then Slocum come along and shot him down in cold blood in the middle of the day while poor old Ace was standing helpless over there in a jail cell. Right now, Slocum is camped just outside of town awaiting his chance to get someone else. It could be any one of us next or any one of our friends and fellow citizens of Whizbang. Amos won't do nothing about it. That's why I called y'all together here."

Out at the bar, Dutch watched the door to the back room. Customers had to call out to him for service. He knew something was wrong back there, but he had kept his nose out of the business of his customers for a long time. This was bothering him, though. At last, Dutch moved down the bar to where a customer stood.

"Run over and get Amos," Dutch said in a low voice. "When you come back, the next one'll be on the house."

The customer left. Dutch glanced from time to time at the closed door to the back room as he swiped at an already clean bar with his towel. A man came in and ordered a beer. Dutch drew it and served it and took the man's money. At last the customer Dutch had sent to get the marshal came back in. Dutch poured him a drink. Then Amos Foss came in and walked to the bar. He was puzzled. Everything seemed peaceful enough. He leaned across the bar and spoke low.

"What's the trouble, Dutch?" he asked.

Dutch leaned across to get close to Foss's ear and speak confidentially. "Hedley, Barber, and Cain," he whispered, "went in the back room. They're the last three of the seven that went out after that cowboy."

"You saw them?" Foss asked, anxious. This was the

break he had been waiting for—someone besides Slocum who could and would name the seven men who had ridden out of town that night.

"Yeah. I saw Ace and six more leave here and go out after the cowboy," said Dutch. "Hedley, Barber, and Cain are the only three of the seven left alive."

Foss looked toward the closed door and started to move, but Dutch reached across the bar and stopped him. "Wait a minute," he said. "Those three have been hanging close all this time, but this is different. There's six of them in there now. Gordon Slick, Murf Richie, and Alf Badger have joined them in there. They're up to something, Amos. It don't look good. I thought you ought to know."

"Thanks, Dutch," Foss said, looking toward the back room.

"Be careful, Amos," Dutch said.

"Don't worry about me," Foss said.

Determined, Foss turned away and walked deliberately across the room. Without hesitating he opened the door to the back room and stepped in. The six men at the long table all jumped and looked at him.

"Well, now," said Foss, "what's going on in here?"

"This here's a private meeting," said Sammy Cain. "I don't recall inviting you to join us neither."

"And just what's the purpose of this private meeting?" Foss asked.

"We don't have to tell you that," said Cain. "This here is a free country, and besides all that, you work for us."

"You wouldn't be in here conspiring to do a killing, would you?" Foss asked. "The killing of that man out there on the hill?"

"We don't know what you're talking about," Cain said. "Get on out of here and leave us alone. This is a business meeting."

"Because I happen to know," Foss went on, "that you three—Sammy, Chunk, Doby—were part of the gang that killed that cowboy, Harley Duggan. I have it from two different sources now. That also means that you three are the ones that Slocum means to kill, and likely that also means that you're in here trying to figure out how to stop him. You're trying to enlist some help, I see. Now I suggest that you three who didn't have a thing to do with all this just get the hell out of here and not get involved. Get on out before you get yourselves into trouble. You others are coming along to the jailhouse with me. You're under arrest for suspicion of murder."

From his place at the far end of the table to Foss's right, Gordon Slick pulled a revolver before Foss knew what was happening, and he snapped off a quick shot. The bullet smashed into Foss's right shoulder, stunning him and crippling his right arm. Foss tried in vain to reach across with his left hand for the six-gun that was hanging at his right side, but two men got up quick and took hold of him.

"You didn't need to shoot Amos," Richie said. "He's our lawman."

"He won't be for much longer," Slick said. "He's arresting all the wrong folks around here."

"But you just shot—"

"Hell, it's all right," said Cain. "He ain't killed. Get someone out there to take him over to Doc's. Hey, get his gun first."

The two men holding onto Foss passed him on to two others out in the big room. Then they ducked back inside and shut the door again.

"Ain't nothing to stop us now," Cain said. "You all got guns on you? Let's mount up and go after Slocum."

"Let's go get the son of a bitch," Slick said.

"I'm ready," said Badger.

They all tried to get out the door at the same time, until Cain had to yell at them to back off. Finally they made their way out one at a time, ran through the big room and out into the street. Dutch threw down his towel in disgust and followed.

Slocum heard the shot. It brought almost everyone in town out onto the street. He grabbed his binoculars and stood up to get a better look. In another minute or two he saw some men helping a wounded man out of the Booze Palace. He watched until he could see that the injured man was Foss. He had a shoulder wound. He saw them help the hurt lawman across the street to what he thought must be the doc's office. The crowd milled around for some time after that, but what was of real interest to Slocum was that six men, including the three he wanted, mounted horses and headed out of town in his direction.

This was something he did not expect. The three had recruited extra help, three more, and now all six were riding after him. The law was immobilized, so it was Slocum against the six. He didn't have time to saddle the Appaloosa. He grabbed his gunbelt and his Winchester both in one hand and vaulted onto the back of the big horse. If he was going to have to fight six, he needed a better vantage point than his little campsite. The six were getting closer. He kicked his horse in the sides and headed west. He was already familiar with the terrain out in that direction, all the way to Halley Lawson's ranch. There was cover out there. There were good spots for sniping away at a group of men. He had done it already before.

He heard shots behind him. They were trying to bring him down. He couldn't turn and fire back, not while riding like this with no saddle. He just didn't have the control he needed for that kind of shooting. He urged the big horse to move faster. Then he heard another shot, and he felt a dull thud in his back. He kept riding. He had to hang on. He had to outdistance those back-shooting bastards back there. He had to outride them and lose them. There was no way he could fight them. Not now.

Slocum wasn't afraid to die, but he sure wasn't ready for it. He didn't want to give in to that bunch, and he had a promise to keep. He had to keep riding and keep riding hard. He knew that he was in danger of riding even the big Appaloosa to death, but he couldn't take a chance. He couldn't slow down. He had to get beyond the reach of the gang that was after him and get them off his trail.

Once that was accomplished, he would still have problems. He had a bullet in his back, and he sure wouldn't be able to tend that himself. He'd have to find a safe place with some friendly help and lay low for a while. He was heading in the right direction. He thought of Halley Lawson. The only real problem would be making sure that he wasn't followed there. He glanced over his shoulder. They were still coming, but he was increasing the distance between them. A few more shots were fired, but none of them came close. They were wasting their ammunition. The distance was too great, especially on racing horses.

He wished that he could stop, dismount, and snap off a couple of shots from his Winchester, but he was afraid that once he got down off the big horse, he wouldn't be able to mount him again. Besides, he wasn't even sure that he'd be able to lift the rifle to his shoulder. He was feeling numb from his waist down. He had to keep riding.

10

The gang saw Slocum turn between two hills and ride down into a valley. They raced after him, but when they reached the middle of the valley, he was nowhere to be seen. They reined in, and their horses stamped around nervously. The six men looked around themselves in all directions. They could see neither horse nor man.

"Where the hell did he go?" Richie shouted.

"He could be anywhere in them hills," said Cain.

"That goddamn spotty-assed horse of his is the fastest son of a bitch I ever seen," said Badger.

"Well," said Cain, "our horses are worn out. If we go on like we been, we'll kill them, and then we'll be walking home."

"Maybe we can slow our pace and still trail after him," said Richie. "He has to stop sometime. Even that horse of his can't run like that forever."

"I don't see no sign," said Slick. "What do you aim to trail?"

"Hell," said Cain, "we might just as well go home. The way I see it, he knows now that the whole damn town is after him. Likely he won't show hisself around these parts again."

"More likely," Badger said, "he'll be dead before dark. I put a rifle bullet smack in his back. If that don't kill him outright, he'll bleed to death out here. He's prob'ly crawled in a hole to hide, and he'll just lay in there and bleed to death."

"Alf's right," said Gordon Slick. "I could tell when his slug hit Slocum's back. He won't live much longer."

"All right," said Cain, "we'll rest our horses a bit. Then we'll head back."

Millicent hurried over to the doc's office. When she went in, Dutch was already there. Doc was wrapping a bandage around Foss's shoulder. "How bad is it?" she asked.

"It won't kill him," Doc said, "but he won't be using that arm much for quite a spell neither."

"What are we going to do, Amos?" Dutch asked. "It's like the whole town has turned outlaw."

"I don't know, Dutch," said Amos, wincing a little from the pain in his shoulder. "I sure can't stand up to them. Not now. We know already that they'll shoot. I arrested the three that's left from the seven man lynch mob that started all this. I didn't even have a gun out. One of them shot me. Not one of the original three, but one of the new ones. I think it was Gordon, but I'm not sure."

"Gordon Slick?" Millicent asked.

"Yeah," said Foss. "I think it was him."

"They've gone crazy," Dutch said. "Maybe I should ride over to Springtown for help."

"If they were to spot you leaving town they'd kill you," Foss said. "Don't try it."

"But we can't just let them get away with this," Millicent said. "They've got to be stopped."

"I tried," Foss said, "and I'll try again, but I won't be much use if they resist. About all I can do now is talk to them."

"Amos," Dutch said, "I should have come to you sooner. Maybe I could have stopped some of this. I'm ashamed of myself for keeping my mouth shut. Hell, I should have tried to stop those seven from going out there that first night."

"It wouldn't have done any good, Dutch," Foss said.

"Don't blame yourself, and don't put yourself in any danger. Just go on back to work now. And thanks, Dutch."

Dutch left the room, his head still hanging. Millicent stepped in closer to Foss. Doc finished wrapping the shoulder and stepped back. "That's all I can do for now," he said. "Just try to get some rest and get your strength back. You lost considerable blood."

Foss got down off the table and stood on his feet, but he was a bit wobbly. Millicent took hold of his good arm. "Let me help you," she said.

"I'll just walk back over to my office," Foss said. "I can rest on one of the cell cots."

"I think you could rest better where there's someone to look out for you," she said. "We'll go to my place. Thank you, Doc."

She walked him to Millicent's Eatery, through the business part of the building and into her private back rooms. Then she put him on her bed and pulled off his boots. "Is there anything I can do for you?" she asked. "Or would you rather just try to get some sleep?"

"You got any whiskey?" he asked.

"Sure," she said.

"Just a shot," he said. "Then I think I'll sleep."

Slocum watched as the six riders turned around and headed back toward Whizbang. He knew that he'd lost them. He also figured they thought that he would die of his wound anyhow and therefore wasn't worth searching for. Well, by God, he'd show them. He'd surprise the hell out of them. He would, that is, if he could keep himself from passing out. He was feeling light-headed and a little dizzy. He knew that he had lost blood, a lot of blood. He did not know if he was still bleeding. A man could bleed to death from just a little wound if he had no way of stopping the flow of blood. He tried to think of something he could do.

He reached around behind his back searching for the bullet hole, and he winced with pain when he found it. At least he knew he could reach it. The question then was what to do about it. He waited until the riders were well on their way. Then he rode back down into the valley. The hillsides on each side of the valley were lined with thick woods. Slocum rode along the edge of the woods looking at the crotches of trees until he spotted one that was filled with spiderweb.

He rode over to the tree and grabbed a handful of the thick web. A huge yellow spider with black spots ran from the disturbance. Slocum looked at the stuff in his hand to make sure there were no live creatures or fly bodies in it. It looked fairly clean. He reached back around his back again and found the bullet hole. Then he jammed the web into and around the hole. It might help.

When Amos Foss woke up it was late in the evening. He could tell, for not much light was coming in through the windows. His shoulder and arm hurt like hell, and he was hungry. He was ravenous. He wasn't awake long before Millicent came back in. She had just gotten rid of her last customers for the day, locked up, and come back to check on him.

"You hungry?" she asked.

"I sure am," he said. "I feel like I could eat a half a cow."

"Well, it's not half a cow," she said, "but I've got a good-sized beefsteak ready for you. I thought you might need it. Just a minute."

She left his side for a brief time and returned with a large platter of food. She helped Foss sit up and get comfortable, then placed the tray on his thighs. He dug right into the steak. She smiled at him. Since the death of her husband, he was only the second man she had allowed into her private rooms. Seeing him hurt and watching him eat, feeling like his nurse, she wondered if she had cut him off too abruptly the last time they had talked.

"Amos," she said, "don't answer me till you're done eating, but I've something to say to you. The last time we talked, I think you wanted to say something to me. I stopped you. Right now I wish I hadn't. If you still want to say it—whatever it was—well, I won't stop you again. That's all I want to say. I'm going to get you some coffee now. I'll be right back."

When she came back with the coffee, he had finished the meal. She took the dirty platter away and put the coffee cup on the tray. He thanked her, picked up the cup, and took a sip. "That's good," he said. "The food was good, too."

"I'm glad you liked it," she said.

"What I was going to say to you the other day," he said, "well, I was going to say that I was just hoping that you weren't taken too much with Slocum. I been admiring you for some time, but I hadn't got up the courage to say anything. I guess what I want to say is that I'd like to come courting—if that's all right with you."

"It's all right with me, Amos," she said. "It's just fine."

"Oh, that's just great," he said. "That's wonderful. I, uh, I guess I'd better be getting along. It'll be late soon, and you'll be wanting to get ready for bed."

He had started to sit up farther, but she stopped him.

"You stay right there, Amos," she said. "I want you here where I can hear you holler if you need anything."

"But I'm in your bed," he protested.

"Just stay there," she said. "I'll be fine. Believe me."

Slocum woke up on the edge of a creek bed early the next morning. He could barely remember how he had gotten there. His horse was grazing nearby. He felt numb and sore. Then he tried to move, and sharp pains shot through his body. He tried to gather his wits about him. He knew he was hurt, and he knew he was weak. He knew he had to get himself up and get moving. He had to get some help. He forced himself and ground his teeth through the pain as he rolled over and got to his hands and knees. Then slowly he stood. His legs were weak and wobbly. He thought he was going to fall, but he didn't. He just stood still for a moment, trying to get used to it.

He called to his horse, and it responded by raising its head and giving a nicker.

"Come here," he said. "Come on."

The big horse stamped his feet. Slocum started moving toward the stallion, but then he noticed his guns on the ground near where he had been lying. He had to turn and go out of his way for them. He had to get them, though. As he took slow and careful steps toward the weapons, he was worrying about how he would manage bending over to retrieve them, and how, if he managed to bend over, he would get back up again.

At last he was standing over the guns. Keeping his back as straight as possible, he bent his knees, finally getting down on one. Still he had to lean forward some to pick up the guns. It hurt like hell, but he got them in his grasp. Slowly he straightened his back again, and slowly he stood up. He waited and took a few deep breaths, then turned to face the horse again. It seemed miles away. "Come on over here, big boy," he said. "Come on." Even his voice was weak.

He took slow and easy steps toward the horse, talking to it and encouraging it with each step, and his mind asked him how, even if he got close enough, he thought he would manage to get back up on that large animal's back. He tried not to think about that. The first problem was getting close to the horse. Once there, he would worry over the next problem. "Come on," he said. "Come here to me."

Then suddenly the Appaloosa threw up his head and whinnied. He turned and trotted to Slocum's side. For an instand Slocum was afraid the horse might bump into him and knock him over, but it did not. It turned smartly and stopped in just the right position for a mount. But how was he to mount it? There was no saddle, therefore no stirrups, and Slocum's back was causing him all kinds of pain. When he was healthy, he could easily mount a bareback horse, even the big Appaloosa, but not in the shape he was in.

He put a hand on the horse's neck and gripped a handful of mane. Then he urged it forward slowly and walked along beside. It was easier to walk with the horse as a crutch, but it was still slow, and it would exhaust him soon. Looking around as they moved along, he saw a rock sticking up out of the ground ahead. The exposed portion was about as high as Slocum's knees. Maybe a little higher. He guided the Appaloosa over to the rock, then used it as stool to climb on.

It still wasn't easy, and it hurt a lot, but he managed to get aboard that way. Now he could ride. He turned the horse's head toward the Lawson ranch, the only place he knew of to go for help.

When Millicent went to unlock her place of business that morning, Foss decided that he would get up and go out into the eatery for his breakfast. He was concerned about Millicent's image in the community, and he did not want to stay in her chambers any longer. She told him that she would bring his breakfast to him, but he insisted on going out. She gave in and walked him to a table. Then she started the morning coffee and stoked up the fire under her griddle. She unlocked her door.

It was only a few minutes before customers started coming in. The first few greeted Foss and asked about his condition. No one seemed to be suspicious of where he had spent the night. They just assumed that he had come in for breakfast before they did. Then Sammy Cain, Chunk Hedley, and Murf Richie came in. They walked directly to the table where Foss was sitting.

"Glad to see you up and around, Amos," Cain said. "I never meant for you to get hurt."

"You're still under arrest, Sammy," said Foss.

"You're in no position to try to do anything about that now," Cain said.

Millicent saw what was going on and hurried over to the table.

"Don't start any trouble in here," she said. "Besides, he's hurt."

"No trouble, ma'am," said Richie. "We're here on official business."

"What business?" Foss asked.

"Why, Amos," said Cain, "you know that we're all on the town council. Well, we had us a meeting last night, and we all voted. It's official. You've been fired. We come to tell you and to get your badge."

"How can you fire him?" Millicent asked. "Just like that?"

"It's all right," Foss said. "They can do it all right."

He pulled the badge off his vest with his left hand and tossed it on the table. Cain picked it up.

"What's the official reason?" Foss asked. "Do you mind telling me?"

"Dereliction of duty," said Cain. "Don't mind at all."

"You locked up Ace and got him killed," said Hedley. "You're lucky we ain't charging you on that."

"And you refused to arrest that Slocum," Richie said. "It's all in the record if you decide to make a protest."

"I won't make any protest," Foss said. "You hired me, and now you've fired me. I never was one to hang around where I wasn't wanted."

"Well," said Cain. "That's that. See you around."

The three town council members turned and walked over to a table and took seats.

"We'd like to order some breakfast here, ma'am," Hedley said.

Millicent pointed to a sign over her counter. "Not in here," she said. The sign read, "We Reserve the Right to Refuse Service to Anyone."

"Hell," said Cain, pushing back his chair, "let's get out of here. The food ain't no good anyhow. And the company's worse."

The three left. Millicent sat down beside Foss.

"They make me so mad," she said. "If I had a gun—"

"Calm down, Millicent," Foss said. "They're not worth it."

"Amos," she asked, "what will you do?"

"I haven't had time to figure that out yet," he said, "but like I said to those skunks, I won't stay where I'm not wanted."

"You can't leave," she said. "Not yet. "You're not well enough to travel."

"I won't do anything without telling you first, Millicent," he said. "I promise you that. Right now I'm keeping you from your work. Go on now. Don't worry about me. I'll be all right."

At the door, Cain, the last to leave, paused. He turned back toward Foss and Millicent. Wanting to get in the last jab, he said, "Oh, by the way. We got that Slocum."

"What do you mean by that?" said Foss.

"We killed him," Cain said. "Deader'n hell. Whizbang's troubles are all over."

"Oh, God," Millicent said.

"Where's the body?" asked Foss.

"Oh, it's out in the wilderness somewhere," Cain said. "Last we seen of him, he was wobbling around on his horse with a bullet in his back. See y'all around."

"Oh, Amos," said Millicent.

"Try not to worry," Foss said. "They might not have killed him. If they didn't bring in a body to gloat over, he might be all right."

It was late evening when the big Appaloosa rode up to Halley Lawson's front porch with Slocum draped over his neck looking more dead than alive. Halley was at the corral, and she knew the horse at once. She saw the man on his back, and she ran to them as fast as she could.

"John," she said. "John. What happened?"

In a barely audible voice, Slocum said, "Bullet in my back."

She reached up to take hold of him and helped him down. When his feet hit the ground, he nearly fell, but she held him up and took him inside.

"Hide my horse," he said.

"That'll wait," she said. "Let me take a look at that bullet hole."

"No," he said. "Hide my horse. I'll wait."

She went out to do as he had told her, and when she returned, she found him lying face down on her bed. The back of his shirt was covered with blood and dirt. She took hold of its tail and pulled it up as far as she could.

He groaned as the shirt was ripped loose from the crusted blood on his back.

"That's ugly enough," she said.

"Can you dig it out of me?" he asked.

11

Halley got out a bottle of good whiskey and uncorked it. She handed Slocum the bottle, and even though his position hampered him a bit, he took several sideways gulps out of it. It burned his throat going down, and it fuzzied his head. That was what he wanted it to do. He put the bottle on the floor. Lying on his stomach the way he was with his arm dangling off the edge of the bed, he could reach it whenever he felt the need.

"Go on," he said.

She took out a short knife, and without hesitation, started digging into the wound like an experienced surgeon. Slocum winced and growled between his clenched teeth. He squeezed his fists closed so hard that his knuckles turned white. It hurt like hell, the digging and probing in raw flesh. There was nothing for him to do, though, but lie still there and take it, and he knew that. The damned slug had to be taken out. He drooled and slobbered onto the sheet. He could feel the side of his face lying in his own spit. At long last, blessedly, the painful digging stopped. He lay still and took several deep breaths. Then he reached for the bottle and took a few more gulps of precious whiskey. He put the bottle back down on the floor.

"Okay," he said. "Go on. I'm ready."

"I got it out," she said.

"Already?" he said. "You're done?"

"It wasn't in very deep," she said. "Thank God for that. It was awful close to your backbone though. Too close for comfort. Hand me that bottle, will you?"

Slocum picked up the bottle again and held it out for her. She took it, took a long drink, and then poured the hole in his back full of the fiery liquid. He yelled out loud. "Ah, goddamn," he said. "That's worse than the digging. Oh. Son of a bitch."

"It's the same stuff you been pouring inside you all along," she said. "It shouldn't hurt you none. Hell, you oughta be used to it."

"Shit," he said.

"Just be still," she said. "I'll get some bandage."

She stood up and walked away to gather up what she needed for dressing the wound, and by the time she got back, he was out cold. Asleep? she wondered. Or passed out from the pain—or the whiskey? She wasn't sure, but she thought that it was just as well no matter what the cause. Let him sleep awhile. It would do him good.

Back in Whizbang, the original three conspirators sat together in the Booze Palace drinking whiskey. Cain was surly. The other two were nervous. Hedley downed a shot-glass full of whiskey and poured himself another.

"I ain't at all sure that Slocum's dead," he said.

"He got a fucking bullet in his back," said Barber. "Didn't he? And riding bareback like that. Trying to hold on to that big-ass horse with a bullet in his back? Shit. He's dead all right. Deader'n shit."

"Sammy," said Hedley, "what do you think? Is he dead? Is Slocum dead, or is he going to come back after us again? What do you think?"

"I think Slocum's the least of our worries right now," said Cain.

"Well, what do you mean?" Hedley asked. "What do you mean by that? If he's alive and he still wants to kill us, that's a pretty big worry, I'd say. Hell, he's killed three already. Four maybe, if we count Ace."

"If he's alive, he's out of commission," said Cain. "He won't be getting around much with that bullet in his back. Not for a while. But right here in town we got ourselves a goddamned ex-lawman who knows every damned thing that happened. He's our main worry now. Not Slocum."

"Amos?" asked Barber.

"Amos Foss," Cain said. "The one and only former upstanding town marshal of our fair town. Honest, loyal, and a pain in the ass."

"We fired his ass," Hedley said.

"He still knows the story," said Cain, "and now that old Slick went and shot him, he's likely some pissed at us. He can't arrest us no more. You're right about that. We fired him. And the shape his shoulder is in, he can't shoot it out with us. But he can sure as hell tell what he knows. He can go out of town and find a U.S. marshal or something. He can spread the word around town and turn the rest of the citizens against us."

"We don't want none of that to happen," said Hedley.

"No way," said Barber.

"What are we going to do?" asked Hedley. "How do we stop him?"

"Kill him?" Barber whispered.

"How can we do it?" Hedley asked.

"Well," said Cain, "I got an idea. You got the guts?"

"For what?" Barber asked.

"You know," Cain said, "Amos lives in a room right there in back of the jailhouse."

Millicent went to the back room at the jail, the room that served as Amos Foss's living quarters, and packed up his few personal belongings. He had told her what he wanted. She was coming out the front of the office with her bundle when Gordon Slick stopped her by blocking her path. He looked at her with a lecherous grin on his long thin face. He reached out and fingered the bundle in her hands, and she pulled back from him.

"What you got there, girlie?" he asked. "What's so precious you don't want me touching it? Huh?"

"If it's any of your business," she said, "which it really isn't, I have Amos Foss's personal belongings here. He asked me to get them for him."

"Maybe I had ought to take a look there to make sure that you ain't stealing nothing," Slick said. "I mean, being as how we ain't got no law in town just now. No offense."

"Maybe you ought to keep your filthy hands to yourself," said Millicent. "And you are offensive. You have no more business checking up on me than I would have checking up on you. Now get out of my way."

Slick didn't move. His grin grew wider and more lurid. He licked his lips and rubbed the inside of his thigh with his palm.

"Hey," he said, "that's a bargain. You can search all over my body anytime you feel like doing it."

"I'd have to wear a pair of gloves and use a ten-foot pole," she said. "Let me by."

"Haw, haw, haw. I reckon she told you," someone guffawed. Slick looked over his shoulder to see Murf Richie standing there.

"Murf," he said, his face flushing. "When the hell did you sneak up there?"

"Just long enough ago to hear a little bit," said Richie. "Let the lady by, Gordie. She don't look none too dangerous to me."

Slick hesitated. He looked around, and the streets were busy. There were people passing by within earshot.

"Let her go," Richie said.

Slick stepped aside, scowling, and Millicent hurried on, her nose in the air.

"Hell," said Slick, "I was just funning with her. That's all."

Richie stepped up close and spoke low. "Well, watch it," he said. "Didn't look to me like she thought it was much fun. Now listen. We teamed up with them vigilantes, didn't we? They upholds the law, you know. Now that Amos is fired, we got to act law-abiding. That's what this is all about. Someone has got to maintain law and order around here, and we can't have any of us acting like bullies. You know?"

"Ah, fuck you, Murf," said Slick. "Come on. Buy me a drink."

Chunk Hedley and Doby Barber were both leaning in close to Sammy Cain when Gordon Slick and Murf Richie stepped into the saloon. "How we going to do it, Sammy?" Hedley asked. Cain saw the other two walk in, and he saw that they had spotted him and his companions. They were coming toward them.

"Shut up," he said to Hedley. "We got company coming."

"But they're with us, ain't they?" asked Hedley.

"Some things we got to keep just to ourselves," Cain said. "Not a goddamn word."

Slick and Richie walked over to join the over three, bringing their own bottle and glasses. They pulled out chairs and sat down. "So what's up here with you all?" Slick asked.

"We just been taking bets on whether Slocum's dead or alive," said Cain. "What do you think?"

"Hell," Slick said, "with that bullet in his back and him riding bareback like he was and way out in the middle of nowhere, my guess is that he eventually just slid down off that big horse's back and lay there bleeding to death. It's been long enough now that he'd done had it."

"You think he's dead then?" Hedley asked.

"I reckon that's what I said," Slick answered. "Now, I got a question for you hotshot town council members. What are you going to do about appointing a new town marshal? You give that any thought yet?"

"Well, no, we ain't," Cain said. "Not really. It's something we'll have to take up at a meeting real soon though."

"When you have that meeting—real soon—think about me," said Slick. "I'm available, and I'm good."

"You quit your job?" Cain asked.

"For a good job like town marshal," said Slick, "I'd quit my job in a minute. Right now."

"You ain't actually quit it yet then?" said Cain.

"No," said Slick, "but that ain't no problem. Like I said, I'll quit it in a minute for the marshal's job."

"Well," Cain said, "we'll sure keep it in mind."

"Do more than that," Slick said. "Bring it up at the meeting. For sure. I'm serious about this. Maybe I had ought to be there to tell the rest of the council how interested I am. You reckon I ought to be there?"

"I'll check on it and let you know," Cain said.

It was nearly midnight when a lone, dark figure moved along close to the backs of the buildings that stood along the main street of Whizbang. The mysterious figure carried a lantern with its flame turned down low. At the corner of each building, he looked furtively around to make sure he was not being observed. Then he hurried on to the back of the next building. At last he arrived at the building that served as marshal's office, jail, and living quarters. Looking all around again, he stepped to the back window of the living quarters. The window was closed and locked.

Looking around, he found a fist-sized rock. He hefted it for size and weight. Then he turned up the flame in the lantern. He heaved the rock through the window, then flung the lantern after it. The flames spread rapidly through the room and soon up the walls. In a few minutes the entire building was ablaze, and the mysterious arsonist had vanished. The building was almost completely lost before anyone even noticed. By the time the alarm had been sounded and people got up and halfway dressed, the old jailhouse was a lost cause. They only stayed up to watch it burn the rest of the way down and to make sure that the flames did not spread to other, nearby buildings.

The next morning the fire was the talk of the town. Millicent was in the street listening to voices in the crowd of curious gawkers.

"What about Amos?" someone said. "Was he a sleeping in there?"

"I don't know," said another. "He always did sleep in there. When did the fire start?"

"Amos wouldn't a been in there," said someone else. "He's been fired."

"Yeah," said yet another, "but had he found hisself another place to live yet? Did anyone look to see if there was a body back yonder?"

Millicent noticed Chunk Hedley standing near the group of talkers and listening intently. They she watched as Gordon Slick walked over to stand beside Hedley. Slick and Hedley both listened to the speculation about the fate of Amos Foss until Slick said, "Hell, he wasn't in there. I seen that Millicent carrying out his stuff yesterday. I bet he's bunking in with her."

Millicent slipped away before Slick noticed her there, but she did take note of the look of disappointment that passed the face of Chunk Hedley. She hurried back to her own quarters behind the eatery. Foss was sitting up in bed.

"Amos," she said, "your old office, the jail, it all burned last night."

"A fire?" he asked.

"I was listening to people in the crowd," she said. "Not many folks know that you'd moved out."

"I guess not," he said. "It's a good thing I did though. I could have been in there."

"That's just what I'm getting at," she said. "When that Chunk Hedley heard that you weren't in there, he looked awfully disappointed."

"I guess he was," said Foss. "I guess—"

He stopped and looked at Millicent. She looked at him, and they read each other's minds.

"You've got to get out of here," she said. "You know that those three were part of the bunch that killed that poor cowboy. You even arrested them. That's why you got shot, and that's why they fired you. It had to be them that started that fire last night. They thought you were still living there. Nobody knows you stayed here with me last night. Well—"

"Well what?" Foss asked.

"That Gordon Slick saw me bringing your things out," Millicent said. "And Murf Richie. I guess they hadn't gotten around to telling the others."

"If they did set that fire—"

"Who else?" Millicent asked. "And if they did, they were trying to get you. And they'll try again."

"If that's true, and they see me trying to leave town," he said, "they'll stop me. I'm sure in no shape to fight them. I have to get out of here, though. I can't have them bringing the fight into your house. I won't have that."

"We'll get out after dark," Millicent said.

"You don't have to—"

"I said we," she said. "And I meant it. Don't you remember what I said. Slick and Richie saw me getting your things. They'll put it all together soon enough, and they might even guess that you told me what you know. You think I'll be safe here by myself?"

"I hadn't thought of that," Foss said. "All right. After dark."

Millicent had everything packed and ready to go by the time the wagon rolled up in back of her quarters. The lights were all out, and she left them that way. She opened the back door and stepped outside carrying a stuffed bag.

"Here, let me get that for you, ma'am," said the driver of the wagon.

"Thanks, Shorty," she said. "There's more."

She stepped back inside for a moment, then re-emerged with both hands full. She and Shorty threw the things into the back of the wagon. Amos Foss stepped out. He was carrying a Henry rifle in his left hand, and his gunbelt with a Colt in it was draped around his left shoulder. He climbed onto the wagon seat. Millicent closed the back door and locked it. Then she climbed up after him. Foss looked down at Shorty.

"Thanks," he said. "I won't forget this."

"Just get out of town safe, Amos," Shorty said. "And you too, ma'am. And don't worry. I'll folly after you for a ways and wipe out your tracks."

"Thanks, old friend," Foss said.

With Millicent handling the reins, the wagon and team moved slowly along the back of the main street buildings. It seemed to take forever, and Millicent and Foss each thought they were making enough noise to wake up the entire population of Whizbang, but soon they were out of town. Foss kept looking over his shoulder to see if there was any pursuit, even any sign of anyone observing their movements. He saw none.

"I think we made it," he said. "Keep moving slow though. This is a rough road. It's worse in the dark. Just let the horses pick their way."

"Yeah," she said. "I know."

"I'm ashamed to be so helpless," he said.

"Hush," she said. "Don't you worry about it. By the time they figure out what happened, we'll be long gone."

Slocum slept in fits. When he woke up, his back hurt him something fierce. He would reach for the bottle and take another slug out of it. If he tried to stay drunk enough, he figured, maybe it wouldn't hurt so much. But when he slept, he dreamed. He dreamed of better times—fun, friendly times with Harley. He dreamed of drinking with Harley, of chasing women with Harley, of fighting side by side with Harley. Those were good dreams. But he also dreamed of Harley with a rope around his neck, Harley being strangled, tortured to death, and Slocum off somewhere having a good time. Those were the worst kind of nightmares, and from them, he awoke in a sweat, his eyes wide with terror.

And he dreamed of chasing and shooting and killing with seven men, then six, then five, then four, then three, and then again with six. He saw their faces. He repeated their names, all but the last three. Those he did not know. He dreamed of watching over a town from a small camp, and he dreamed of the camp under attack, of bullets whizzing all around him, and of one crashing into his back. He dreamed of a sharp knife carving on his back. He woke up, and he drank some more.

12

Foss figured that if they were followed, which was likely, Cain and the others would expect them to head north to Springtown. That would be the first direction in which pursuers would try to pick up a trail. If Shorty had done a good job wiping out their tracks out of town, it would be a while before anyone would think of looking west, especially for a wagon. Now and then, Foss had Millicent stop the wagon, and they got out to wipe out their trail. Then he had an even better idea. He had Millicent turn north for a few miles, as if they had headed west to fool any trackers, then turned back toward Springtown. After a few miles of this, they tied heavy brush onto the back of the wagon to wipe out the tracks as they were made. Then they turned back west.

Foss thought that he had come up with every way possible to throw off any pursuit that might be coming. Even so, he occasionally looked back to see if anyone might be following. He was certain that they would try. He knew too much on those three respectable citizens, and he also had a charge to file on a fourth, Gordon Slick. They would try to eliminate him. Of that, he was certain.

And Millicent was in danger, too. As she had pointed out to him, it made sense to think that the criminals would surmise that Foss had confided in her. They would therefore think that she knew all that he knew. She would have to be gotten rid of, too, in order to assure their own safety. Foss thought about the upstanding citizens of Whizbang that he had been working for all these years, and he asked himself if those years had all been wasted. What kind of people had he been protecting? How had they been using the law to their own advantage? How had they been using him as their tool?

Slick hurried to find Sammy Cain. He found him at work in his gunsmith shop. When Slick rushed in the door, Cain looked up from his work and saw that Slick was agitated about something. He laid aside the Merwin and Hulbert Company revolver he was working on and stood up.

"Sammy," Slick said, "we got a problem."

"What is it?" Cain asked.

"Amos Foss is gone," Slick said, "and that Millicent gal is with him."

"Gone?" Cain said. "Where the hell did they go?"

"Damned if I know," said Slick, "but I heard folks grumbling about Millicent's Eatery being locked up tight this morning, so I went over there to investigate. I banged around front and back and never got no answer, so I busted in the back door. There ain't no sign of neither one of them anywhere in town."

"Goddamn it," Cain said.

"You know what that means, don't you?" said Slick. "Amos arrested you and Doby and Chunk. Then I shot him. He could report all that to the county sheriff or a U.S. marshal, and we could have all kinds of law on our ass."

"I know. I know," Cain said. "Damn it to hell. Get all the boys together and let's find them."

"Looks to me like they headed out west," Murf Richie said. "Someone tried to wipe out the tracks, and almost done it too, but looky here. A wagon headed west."

"How do we know they was in a wagon?" Slick asked.

"It just makes sense," said Richie. "With Amos's shoulder stove up the way it is. And they packed out their clothes and stuff."

"But why would they head west?" Cain asked. "If they're going to the law, they'd have to head north to Springtown."

"This here wagon headed west," Richie said, "and we never seen no other sign of anyone leaving town last night."

"All right, shit, let's go," Cain said, and the six riders rode hard on the trail west out of Whizbang. They rode hard until they lost the trail. Then they had to slow down and search for it again. This happened to them several times, but still they rode west. About noon, they saw where the wagon had turned north.

"Goddamn it!" Cain shouted. "I was right all along. They're headed for Springtown. Come on. Maybe we can head them off."

The six riders turned northwest to try to get ahead of their prey somewhere along the road from Whizbang to Springtown.

Slocum sat up the second day, in spite of Halley's protests. Now and then he got up to walk around. The wound in his back still caused him some pain, and he was stiff all over, but he figured the fastest way to get back in shape was to start doing everything he could do. The way Slocum thought, the only thing laying around did for a man was to make him stiff and useless. He walked to the outhouse when he needed to go, and he got up to sit at the table for his meals. He cleaned his Colt and his Winchester. Toward the afternoon, he even walked out to the far pen in the brush where Halley had secreted his Appaloosa, and he gave the big stallion a rubdown.

"You sure as hell saved my ass, old partner," he said.

When he went back into the house, Halley was scowling at him. "You don't take it easy, you're going to overdo it," she said. "Then you might be flat on your back for a good long spell."

"I'll be all right," he said. "Hell, I'm taking it easy. All I'm doing is walking around a little bit."

"Sit down and have some coffee," she said. She put the cup of steaming black liquid on the table and he sat there.

"Thanks," he said.

"I got to ride out and check on some cows," she said. "Can I trust you to behave yourself while I'm gone?"

"I won't do a damn thing but maybe get up to pour myself some more coffee now and then," he said.

"You promise me?" she asked.

"I might smoke a cigar," he said. "Got them right here in my pocket. Matches, too."

"All right," she said. She put an empty tin can on the table for him to use as an ashtray. "I'll get back here fast as I can."

The right back-end corner of the wagon took a sudden drop and a hard bounce, and the shock of its landing sent shards of pain shooting through Amos Foss's body. Millicent fought the horses with the reins and managed to get them stopped and calmed.

"What happened?" she asked.

Foss turned to look. He saw the wheel spinning off to the right.

"We lost a wheel," he said.

"Oh, no," she said.

They both climbed down, Foss slowly and painfully. Then they walked back to inspect the axle. "Can it be fixed?" she asked.

"Yeah," he said. "If the wheel's all right."

He turned to walk after the wheel, and then he bent to pick it up with his left hand. As he straightened, he winced with pain.

"Here," Millicent said, "let me have that."

She took the wheel away from him and rolled it back to the wagon. Foss followed her.

"The only problem is," he said, "we have to lift the wagon in order to get the wheel back on. I don't think I can do it."

"Well, I can try," she said.

"If you can lift it," he said, "maybe I can get the wheel on with my left hand."

Millicent backed up to the tailgate of the wagon. She bent her knees and took hold of the wagon with both hands. Then she strained to straighten her legs. She got it up a little, but not nearly enough. She dropped it again.

"It's no use," Foss said.

"Wait," she said. "I'll try again."

Foss moved in beside her and tried to help her out using only his left hand, but the pain that shot through his body was too much for him. He had to give it up. Millicent kept straining. She had the wagon lifted a few inches, and Foss happened to notice something underneath.

"Let it down," he said.

She did. Then she stood panting for breath.

"What's wrong?" she asked him.

"It's no use," he said. "The axle's broke underneath. We'll have to unhitch the horses and try to ride them."

"What about all our things?" she asked.

"We'll pack what we can on the horses with us," he said. "We'd best do that while they're still hitched."

Working together, they managed to pack everything they had brought onto the backs of the two horses and still leave room to mount them. They unhitched one horse, led it to the side of the wagon, and tied it there. Then they did the same with the second horse. Millicent and Foss then climbed into the wagon. She watched while Foss managed to step out of the wagon bed and mount the horse. Then she untied it and handed him the line.

"You all right?" she asked.

"I'll make it," he said.

Millicent moved across the wagon bed to mount the other horse. She climbed on its back, then reached down to untie it. Then she turned it to face west. "Well," she said, "are we ready to go?"

"As ready as we'll ever be," Foss said.

They started riding. Foss didn't say anything, but he knew that the going would be slow and the bareback riding would be rough on their legs and asses. He looked at Millicent with a worried expression.

"I should never have let you get involved in this mess," he said.

"Never mind that kind of talk," she said. "I'm in it, and that's all there is to it. We're in it together."

"But I don't even know where we're going," he said.

"Don't worry," she said. "There's something out there somewhere."

Halley was riding along a low ridge and looking down into the valley below. She stopped. There was a broken-down wagon. There were no horses and no human beings in sight. She rode down to inspect the scene, and soon discovered that a wheel had come off, and when the corner of the wagon fell, the axle had broken. There was nothing in the wagon bed. Whoever had been driving must have loaded his goods on the back of one horse and taken the other to ride. She wondered why anyone would be out in this country with a wagon anyhow. She decided to follow the prints of the horses. Whoever it was might be in trouble.

She was riding the little roan mare, and it was fleet of foot, so it didn't take her long to catch up with the two riders on the draft horses. As she rode up behind them, they both turned to see who was coming. Foss and Millicent relaxed when they saw that the rider was a woman. They stopped and allowed Halley to ride up easy beside them.

"Howdy, folks," Halley said. "I saw your wagon back there and figured someone might be in a little trouble."

"Oh, well, thank you," said Millicent. "I don't know how you could help though. The axle broke on our wagon, so all we can do is ride these horses."

"What are you doing way out here alone?" Foss asked.

"I ain't way out nowhere," Halley said. "I just live a few miles over thataway. Say, you've been hurt."

"He's been shot," said Millicent.

"Seems to be a lot of that going around," Halley said. "Who shot you?"

"I was the town marshal of Whizbang," Foss said. "I

arrested three men, and one of their friends shot me. Right after that the town council fired me."

"For trying to arrest someone?" Halley said.

"They were members of the town council," said Foss.

"Say," Halley said, "I went to Whizbang once. It was some time ago, but when I think on it, I recognize you. Yeah. You were the local law all right. I recollect it now. And you, you got a eating place there, don't you?"

"I did," said Millicent. "I left it behind."

"If you don't think I'm being too nosey," Halley said, "did your problem with those men have anything to do with a little ruckus stirred up by a man name of Slocum?"

"It did," said Foss.

"How do you know about that?" asked Millicent.

"Why don't you two come home with me," Halley said. "I'll tell you all about it while we ride. You can rest up at the house, and if you're still of a mind to ride on, maybe I can trade you a couple of good riding horses for these nags you're on. Get you some saddles, too. And we'll get a good meal in you. That ought to help your dispositions some."

"Thank you," said Millicent.

"It sure sounds inviting," Foss said.

Slocum heard the riders coming, and he picked up his Colt. He'd rather have taken up the Winchester, but he wasn't at all sure he could handle it. He moved quickly to the window, pangs running through his body in answer to the hasty movements. He winced with the pain, but he sidled up to the window and looked out. He saw three riders coming. He thumbed back the hammer and waited. Soon, though, he eased the hammer back down. He recognized Halley. A moment later, he saw who she was bringing with her: Millicent and Amos Foss. What the hell, he thought. He put the Colt back in the holster and stepped out onto the porch. When the riders were close enough to hear, he asked, "What the hell brings you two out here?"

• • • •

"You were right all along, Slocum," Foss was saying.

They were seated at the table in Halley's cabin and had just finished a big meal. Millicent had poured refills of coffee all around.

"There's no way to handle that bunch but to go in shooting," Foss continued.

"How'd they come to shoot you?" Slocum asked.

"I got your story confirmed," Foss said. "At least enough of it to arrest the last three men with. The bartender at the saloon saw seven men leave to ride out to your camp. He gave me their names. It matched what you had told me, so I arrested the last three of them. They had three new men with them, though, and it was one of them that drew down on me and shot me."

"And then the six of them came at me at my little camp," Slocum said. "Well, they got us both crippled up now. They can relax a spell, I guess.

"Hell," said Foss, "they think you're dead."

Slocum grinned. "That's even better," he said. "Soon as I've healed up a bit, I'll just ghost right in on them."

"You're going back?" Millicent said.

"I ain't done yet," said Slocum. "Yeah. I mean to go back and finish what I started."

"If I'm fit for it by the time you are," said Foss, "I'd like to go with you."

"That's all right with me," said Slocum. "But you take the three new ones. Leave the others to me."

"I think you're both crazy," Millicent said. She stood up and flounced away from the table. Halley was about to go outside. "Where are you going?" Millicent asked.

"Got to feed my critters," said Halley.

"Can I help?" said Millicent.

She followed Halley outside, leaving Slocum and Foss sitting alone together at the table. Slocum took two cigars out of his pocket and offered one to Foss. Foss accepted, and Slocum struck a match on the underside of the table. He held it out for Foss, and when Foss had his smoke going, Slocum lit his own. He flicked out the match and dropped it in the tin can.

"You know who all these men are," he said. "You know where they live?"

"Yeah," said Foss. "I know where they live."

"Do any of them live close to each other?" Slocum asked.

"No," Foss said. "Not really."

"They got folks living with them?" asked Slocum.

"Alf Badger's got a wife," Foss said. "Murf Richie's got a wife and a couple of kids. Gordon Slick works out on the Crooked S spread, so he lives there with a bunch of cowhands. The rest of them are bachelors and live alone."

"That's good," Slocum said. "What I'd like to do is to get you to draw a map to show me where each one lives. Then we can plan our moves."

"It'll be a while before we're fit to make any moves," said Foss.

"But we can take that time to get ready," Slocum said. "Say, how'd Millicent come to be with you out here anyhow?"

"Oh," said Foss. "Well, I, uh, I had been with her, uh, visiting, and then when I got shot, she took me to her place to tend me. When I got fired, she went over to the office to get my things for me. So when I decided that I'd better get out of town, she said that they might come after her. They might think that I'd told her everything I know, so she wouldn't be safe. That's when I agreed to let her come along."

"Are you and she, uh—"

"We kind of talked about it a little," said Foss, blushing a bit. "We haven't yet actually—well, I haven't yet actually asked her. Things just started happening too fast."

"Yeah," said Slocum. "They sure did."

13

There were four of them now, and they could easily watch for any unwanted company that might come their way. Millicent and Foss had told them how they had laid a false trail to Springtown, and when Halley had come across the two of them, she had seen no sign of any pursuit. Most likely, Cain and the rest had followed the false trail, and they thought that Slocum was dead. So Slocum relaxed a little more, and he brought his big Appaloosa out of hiding. He put it in the corral with the other horses. He had gone out to the corral to see the stallion when Millicent came out of the house and walked over to join him.

"He's a beautiful animal," she said.

"He's been a good partner to me for a long time," Slocum said. "He's a damn good horse."

"Well, of course, I'm no judge," she said, "but I think I've never seen a better one."

"He's as good a horse as I've ever known," Slocum said, rubbing the big animal's neck.

"John," she said, "there's something I want to tell you."

"I'm listening," he said. "I didn't think you came out here to talk about horses."

"Amos wants to marry me," she said.

"He told me," said Slocum. "How do you feel about it?"

"I ran away with him," she said. "I left my business behind. He's a good man, John. I mean to do it."

"That's good," Slocum said. "I think you're doing the right thing. He is a good man, and he'll treat you right. He'll take good care of you. I wish you both a long and happy life together."

"Did you say anything about?—"

"I never said a thing about you and me," Slocum said, "and I never will. Don't you worry your pretty little head about that. Hell, I wouldn't do anything to spoil your chances for a good life. By the way, have you and Amos?—"

"Oh, no," she said, a slight flush on her cheeks. "Amos is a real gentleman. He would never—I'm sorry. I know how that sounded. I didn't mean to—"

"That's all right," Slocum said. "I guess I know that I ain't no gentleman, and I guess I know what you meant. The only thing is, that makes me feel kind of awkward. You know, with us all staying together here, and you and me, well, done what we did, and you and him ain't done it yet, and here you are fixing to get married up. It, well, hell, it just don't seem right somehow. You know what I mean?"

"I know," she said. "I feel the same way. Kind of funny like. I don't know exactly how to say it. But till we get a preacher and make it legal, Amos will never make a move on me like that."

"Well, then," Slocum said, "it looks to me like you're just going to have to make the move on Amos. There ain't nothing else for it. Is there?"

"I guess not," she said. "But John?"

"Yeah?"

"What will he think of me?"

"Well, now, I can't really answer that one for you," he said, "but I'll just say that if he thinks any less of you for it, he ain't half the man I think he is."

It was later that same day when Halley announced that she was going back out to finish the ride around the range she had started the day she ran across Foss and Millicent. She had cut short her ride that day in order to bring them around to the house. Slocum stood up and told her that he'd like to make the ride out with her.

"How come?" she asked.

"I've been idle too long," he said, "and it's time I put a saddle on the back of my stallion again."

"You sure you're up to it?" she asked.

"I got to do it sometime," he said. "I can't just lay around here and get stiff."

"Well," Halley said, "maybe the ride will be good for you at that. We'll start out kind of easy. There ain't all that much to do out there today. I already got a good start on it. Well, hell, let's go then."

They found a saddle in Halley's tackroom that would fit the big horse and saddled it up along with the small roan for Halley to ride. Halley did most of the work. Slocum's back pained him too much to lift a saddle and swing it onto the back of a horse. Ready to mount up, she hesitated and looked over at Slocum.

"Can you climb aboard?" she asked him.

"I'm fixing to find out now," said Slocum. He took hold of the saddlehorn with both hands and raised his left foot slowly up to the stirrup. It hurt a little, but he made it all right. Then he took a deep breath, pulled himself up with his arms, swung his right leg up and over, and settled down in the saddle. "Ah," he sighed. His face was wrinkled with the strain and pain.

"Are you all right?" Halley asked.

"I'm just fine now," he said, lying only a little. "Let's go ride."

They rode out easy, making small talk, choused up a few cows along the way, and finally they reached the abandoned wagon, the end of Halley's previous ride. At that point, Slocum rode around some, looking for any sign that Cain and his cohorts might have followed the wagon tracks. He found none, but then he hadn't really expected to. Then he rode up to the top rise of the highest ground in sight and carefully surveyed the area all around. It seemed that, except for himself and Halley, he was alone in an uninhabited wilderness. In another minute, Halley rode up beside him.

"See anything?" she asked.

"Nothing." he said. "I think we figured it right in the first place. No one's likely to follow us out this way."

"You know," she said, "it does seem that you're clear of them. You could stay here, or you could ride off in any direction, anywhere you wanted. You'd be safe enough. You'd never see nor hear anything from anyone in Whizbang again. It's all over Slocum, if you want it to be. Leave it."

"But you know I can't do that, Halley," he said. "I've got me three more men to kill back there, and I mean to do it. Harley was my partner, and I made him a solemn promise. I have to keep it."

"You might have to kill six men," she said. "Not just three. You heard what Amos and Millicent said, didn't you? And if they got three more to join with them, they might be able to get even more."

"If those other three men get in my way," Slocum said, "I'll deal with them, too, and any others that join with them. I didn't invite them in on this deal, but if they want a part in it, they can have it. Them and like I said, any others that choose to play with Cain. There ain't nothing going to stop me, Halley. Nothing short of killing me."

"Yeah," she said. "Hell, I know that. I know I'm just wasting my breath. And when you've done with all that killing, you'll be on your way to—where, Slocum? Where will you go from here?"

"Oh, hell, I don't know," he said. "I don't very often think that far ahead. Hell, I might just come back here and hang around with you for a spell."

"Ha," she said. "Fat chance of that."

"You never know," he said.

Back at the ranch house, Foss was up and pacing the floor. He'd had his breakfast, and he'd had all the coffee he could drink for a while. His shoulder kept him from riding out with Halley and Slocum, and he was bored with inactivity. He'd seldom been hurt in his career, and a wound was something he did not bear with much patience. The inaction tormented him more than the pain.

Millicent, on the other hand, busied herself with cleaning up after the breakfast, but there was something else on her mind. She knew what she had to do, but she hadn't yet figured out just what her approach would be. Finally, when she could find nothing more around the small house to putter with, and no more excuse to put it off, she walked to the side of the bed and looked at Foss, still pacing.

"Amos," she said.

"Yes?" he said, but he continued pacing.

"Amos," she said, "come here a moment. Can we talk?"

"Of course," he said. He stopped pacing, and he walked over to her side. She sat on the edge of the bed and patted the spot beside her. He sat down a bit nervously. "What is it?" he asked. "Is something bothering you?"

"Amos, did you ever actually ask me to marry you?" she said. "Or did I just kind of get the idea in my head all by myself?"

"Well, I—if I didn't, Millicent," he said, "I meant to. I meant to when the time was right, you know. Well, I'll just go ahead and do it now. Millicent, when we're safely out of this mess we're in, and when I've found myself another way of making a living, will you do me the honor of becoming my wife?"

"Oh, Amos," she said. "Do you really want me, or did I force you into saying that? Tell me the truth now."

"Oh, no, Millicent," he said. "I mean yes. I mean, I want you very much. Millicent, I—I love you. I want you to be my wife."

"Then why should we wait?" she asked him. "Why not go ahead—right now?"

"I don't want to bring my troubles into your life," Foss said. "And you know, I just lost my job."

"Your troubles are my troubles already, Amos," she said, "and believe me, I'm not complaining about that. Not a bit. If I'm to be your wife, that's as it should be. So why should we wait?"

"Well," he said, scratching his head, "when you put it

that way, I guess there's really no reason to wait any longer. I'll change my question. Millicent, will you marry me just as soon as we can find a preacher?"

"Yes, Amos," she said, "I will. I'll marry you just as soon as we get the chance, but I'll go you even one better than that. Since you finally asked me, in my heart and soul, I'm already your wife."

She stood up and stepped around in front of him, and as he watched, fascinated, she slowly unfastened her dress. Then she began stripping off her clothes, a piece at a time, dropping them casually on the floor. She first revealed her proud round breasts, then her shapely hips and thighs, the rest of her long legs, and at last, the dark and moist triangular mound at her crotch was right there before his greedy and almost unbelieving eyes. She stood before him stark naked, ready and willing.

"Oh, my God," he said. "You're so beautiful. Do you really think we ought to do this?"

"I think it would be just fine," she said. "After all, we're promised. It's not our fault there's not a preacher anywhere near."

"You're right," he said. "It's not our fault."

Tentatively, he reached out a trembling left hand. She took it and placed it on the inward curve of her waist. The touch of it thrilled him throughout his entire body. With difficulty, he pulled his eyes away from the thrilling sight that was right before him, and tilted back his head to look up into her face. He thought that he had never seen it look so lovely. She gave a gentle tug and he stood up. She reached her arms around him, and he took her lovely body in his own good left arm and pulled her close to him. They held one another tightly and pressed their lips together.

Slowly Millicent parted her soft wet lips, and when Foss responded, she darted her lively tongue into his eager mouth. Foss could suddenly feel the once flaccid thing that dangled between his legs grow, harden and begin straining and pressing against his jeans in its valiant but vain attempt to stand up straight. As she pressed the full length of her nakedness against him, Millicent felt it, too. She let a hand slide down his back and then move around. She forced it in between their tightly pressed bodies to reach down and press the ready and throbbing tool.

Then she forced herself away from the tight embrace and started to undress Foss. Carefully, because of his injured shoulder, she pulled his shirt off over his head. She tossed it aside, then gave his shoulder a tender touch. She looked up into his eyes. "Did I hurt it?" she asked.

"No," he said. "I'm just fine."

She had him sit back down on the edge of the bed, and then she knelt before him to pull off his boots. Still on the floor, she reached up with both hands, unfastened his trousers and gave them a tug. He lifted his ass enough to allow her to pull them down and off. Freed at last, his anxious cock stood up straight and full and ready for action. Millicent gave it an eager look and then gripped it and gave it a squeeze. Foss thought that it was trying to buck out of her hand. With both hands now, she fondled it, and her fingertips gently tickled the sack of swollen balls that dangled beneath. Finally, she stood up, and she tenderly pushed Foss until he was lying stretched out on his back on the bed.

"Now, just relax," she said. "Don't worry about a thing. I'll take care of everything."

She crawled onto the bed and straddled him like a horse. Taking hold of the engorged cock with one hand, she guided its head into the wet, waiting slot between her legs. Foss gasped with surprised pleasure at the sensation. Slowly then, Millicent lowered herself on him until the entire length of his rod was driven up deep inside her. She sat still a moment luxuriating in the feel of it. Then slowly she moved her hips forward, sliding along the length of it at the same time. She rode back.

"Ah," said Foss. "My God, that's wonderful."

"Yes," she said. "Yes."

She stopped moving her hips and lowered herself until her breasts were pressed against his chest, and she gave him a long, wet kiss. Then she smiled, straightened herself up again and began the motions anew. The slow and easy lovemaking was pleasant enough, but her excitement grew, and she increased the pace. At last she was riding him hard and fast and furious, and by the time she at last reached her climax and stopped to moan out loud in ecstasy, her body was dripping wet with sweat.

"Are you all right?" Foss asked her.

"I've never felt better in my life," she said. "I could do this all day."

"That's a wonderful thought," he said.

"Yes," she said, "isn't it?"

She started her movements once again, and Foss groaned out loud. This time she started at almost full speed and fury, and this time she climaxed quickly, and as she did, and as she sighed out her intense pleasure, Foss felt the pressure behind his cock grow and intensify and then release.

"Ah," he said. "Ah. Oh my God. Oh, my Millicent. I never had anything so great in my life. Millicent, my darling, I love you."

She stretched out her full length against his body. "I love you, too, Amos," she said. "I love you very much."

Slocum and Halley rode up to a clear stream and dismounted to allow their horses a drink and a rest. Halley got down and stretched out on her belly to drink from the stream. At last she lifted her head. "Ah," she said. "That's good water. Good and cold." She shoved herself up on her hands and knees, then turned to sit down. Slocum was standing nearby. It came to her then that his back would not allow him to go through such antics for a drink of water. She stood up and walked over to his big Appaloosa, taking the canteen off his saddle. She emptied it of its contents, then refilled it with the fresh, cold water. She handed it to him. "Try it," she said.

He took a long drink, and then lowered the canteen. "It is good," he said. "Thanks."

"Rest here a while?" she asked him.

"Sure," he said. "I'm in no hurry to get back."

He looked around until he spotted a huge old tree with

some protruding roots. One large one looked as if it would make a good seat. He walked over to try it out. Sitting on the exposed root, he leaned back against the trunk. It made a comfortable seat. He took out a cigar and lit it.

Halley paced around a bit nervously.

"Sit down," Slocum said. "Relax."

"Hell, I can't," she said. "I'm thinking of all the work I got to do back at the house."

"You got three hands to help you out now," he said. "Both me and Amos Foss are somewhat impaired, but we'll still get the work done faster than you'd have ever got it done just by yourself. And besides all that, well, I'd sure hate for us to walk in and interrupt something back there."

"What?" she said. "You mean—them two back there?"

"They're planning to get hitched," Slocum said, "and they ain't never had the chance to—well, you know what I'm getting at."

"I'll be damned," she said. "So that's why you wanted to come along with me. To leave them two alone for a while."

"That was part of the reason," he said.

"What was the rest of it?" she asked.

"Like I said before," he told her, "I thought it was time I got back in the saddle."

"Anything else?" she said.

"Oh," he said, "I reckon I kind of like your company a bit, too."

She walked over to stand in front of him. She looked down at him for a moment, then suddenly sat down astraddle of his legs. She kissed him long and hard and wet. Then she backed off and looked him in the eyes.

"Well, I kind of like your company, too," she said, "and when you told me what them two was up to back in my house, why, it sort of got me to thinking." She kissed him again. "And the thinking got me horny."

14

Halley was a fine woman—in a whole lot of different ways, and Slocum liked her a lot. He thought that he was beginning to like her too much. He had things to do and places to go. He might settle down for a spell and even actually enjoy it for a while, but he knew that one day he'd wake up with a bad case of the wanderlust. He didn't want to set himself or any woman up for that kind of a fall. He was anxious to get on with his business.

To hurry things along, he threw himself into the ranch work, and at the end of each day, he tried his weapons. He was a little more limber each day, a little closer to normal. At last, he decided that a few more days would do the trick. It would soon be time for him to go back to Whizbang and fulfill the rest of his promise.

And Amos Foss was doing the same thing. He was working a little more each day. It was several days after his arrival on the scene before he could even try his gun hand, and when he first tried it, it was of no use whatsoever. He practiced with his left hand. But after several days of working at it, he was not only becoming fairly proficient with his left, he was also beginning to get back the use of his right.

One evening the two men stood side by side in an open field. At a distance in front of them, tin cans were thrown on the ground. Slocum pulled his Colt and fired five shots. Five cans bounced. Foss pulled his Remington out and fired two shots with his left hand. Two cans bounced. He shifted it to his right hand and fired three more shots. Three cans bounced. Then Slocum picked up his Winchester and put it to his shoulder. He took aim at a can farther away and fired. The can flopped and rolled.

Slocum looked at Foss. "Any day now," he said.

"I'm ready for it," said Foss.

Back at the ranch house, the two men sat down at the table with a bottle and a glass each. Slocum poured the glasses full. Each man picked up his glass and looked at the other. Their faces were stern. They drank. It was a silent but solemn pledge. They knew what had to be done. There was no need to talk about it any more. They also knew that they would ride out the next morning.

The women stood back watching, also knowing what the silent ceremony was all about. They looked at one another without speaking. They knew that the two men would ride out in the morning headed for Whizbang with killing on their minds. They might be successful. They might just get themselves killed. But there was no talking about it. The men had decided, and that was that. Besides, each woman knew that she would have no respect for the man she was worrying about if he chose not to go back.

Slocum chose to sleep outside that night, and Halley joined him, leaving the house and the bed for her two other guests to enjoy. This might be her last chance, she thought, but she kept that thought to herself. She stripped naked in the moonlight and crawled into the bedroll by his side.

"Just hold me," she said. "That's all you have to do."

Inside the house, Foss and Millicent slept soundly in each other's arms.

They rode out early, having said their almost silent good-byes. For a while they rode along side by side in silence. Slocum was on his own Appaloosa. Foss rode a black stal-

lion provided by Halley. Both men wore grim and determined faces. Both men looked straight ahead. They would
have to talk some and relax a little somewhere along the
way. It was a two-day ride back to Whizbang.

With the sun high overhead, they found a nice grassy
spot beside a clear running stream, and they stopped to
make a fire and have a meal. They unsaddled the horses
and let them graze and water on their own. Slocum built
the fire while Foss unpacked some of the foodstuffs Halley
had sent along with them. They had a good meal, almost
like home cooked, and then they drank coffee. Slocum
offered Foss a cigar, and they both smoked.

Then, their cigars gone up in smoke, their small fires
almost burned out, their bellies full of good food and coffee, horses rested, watered and fed, they decided that it
was time to move on. "You ready?" Slocum asked.

"Any time you are," said Foss.

"Then let's hit it," said Slocum.

He stood up and started kicking dirt on the fire. Foss
began packing up the pots and pans. In just a few minutes,
they were ready to saddle the horses. Slocum bent to pick
up his saddle, but he stopped when Foss spoke.

"Riders coming," the ex-lawman said. "Two. From the
south. Driving four extra horses."

Slocum straightened up and looked. "They wouldn't
seem to be Whizbangers," he said. "Not coming from that
direction. But they're headed for us, sure enough. Stay
loose."

Slocum held his Winchester loosely and casually, but
he held it in such a way that he would be able to bring it
into play quickly and easily. He and Foss stood silently
watching the approaching riders and waiting for them to
come in close. When they were near enough to hear a
shout, Slocum stopped them.

"That's close enough," he called out.

The riders slowed and stopped as soon as they could
manage it, but by then they were all within six-gun range
of one another. Slocum didn't like that, but he figured they

had done their best. They were driving four loose horses, after all.

"What can we do for you?" he asked them.

"Why, nothing, really," said the larger of the two men. He and his companion had the look of cowboys. "We just seen some human life over here and thought we'd stop to swap tales. That's all. Just being friendly."

"Ordinarily we don't mind being friendly," Slocum said, "but right now we're in kind of a hurry. Sorry. But we'll be moving along soon as you all ride on your way."

"Well, uh, we kind of like your campsite here," the big wrangler said. "If you're moving on, we'll just settle right here for a spell."

Slocum looked over at Foss. Foss gave a shrug. "It's open country," he said. "By the way, where you two boys headed?"

"I thought you was in too big a hurry to slow down and visit with folks," the big puncher said.

"Maybe we ain't in quite as big a hurry as I thought," said Slocum.

"Well then," said the cowboy, swinging down out of his saddle, "we're just drifting around. Hunting horses. I hear the army's buying all they can get over at Fort Hoopla. Them's nice-looking horses you all got. Where'd you get them?"

"Bought them," said Slocum.

The cowboy sniggered. "Yeah," he said. "Well, we're chasing wild ones. Catch them and break them. Then run them over to Fort Hoopla to sell. It's a living."

"I ain't seen many wild horses in these parts," Slocum said. Something about these two bothered him. The four horses they were driving, for one thing, did not have the look of wild mustangs. He looked closer and saw that they were shod. He also took note of the way the silent cowboy kept looking at his and Foss's mounts. He thought about Halley's stock back at her ranch and how the two women were alone out there. "Which way did you say you were riding?"

"Didn't say," said the talker. "But you're right. Ain't

many wild horses around here. We're thinking about heading west a ways. Try our luck out thataway."

"Hell," said Foss. "I got a soft spot for horse hunters. How long's it been since you boys had a cup of hot coffee?"

The talking cowboy grinned. "Been quite a spell," he said. "A good cup of coffee would just hit the spot. You got some?"

Slocum looked over at Foss, and thought, he's thinking the same way I am. That's good. "We got some," he said. "If you want to build this fire back up, we'll break it out."

The big cowboy nodded at his partner, and the smaller one moved to stir the ashes and throw a few new sticks on the fire. Slocum unpacked the coffeepot and walked over to the big cowboy. He held out the pot. "Fetch some water," he said, "and I'll dig out the coffee grounds."

The cowboy took the pot down to the water's edge, and Slocum went for the coffee. In the meantime, Foss managed to get a closer look at the four "wild" horses the men were driving. He walked over close to Slocum, pretending to help unpack. He pulled out some tin cups, and he spoke to Slocum in a low voice. "One of those wild horses," he said, "is wearing a brand."

"I figured," said Slocum.

They put the coffee on to boil and waited. There was a tension in the air around them. Both Slocum and Foss were suspicious of these men, and the men could tell. Slocum was still thinking of Millicent and Halley alone at the ranch to the west. The horse thieves—Slocum had decided that these men were such—were headed west. At least that's what the talker had said. Slocum had half a mind to just kill them. Just in case. But he waited.

"You keep studying our horses," Slocum said.

"They're good-looking horses," said the talker. "Now, horses like that would bring a good price over at the fort."

"If someone was to take them over there to sell," Slocum said.

The cowboy grinned. "Yeah," he said. "That's what I

meant. You wouldn't have a mind to sell them, would you?"

"Sell them to you?" Slocum asked.

The cowboy shrugged.

"And then walk out of here?" Foss added.

"If you had any money," said Slocum, "you wouldn't be out here chasing horses. Would you?"

"I reckon not," the cowboy said. "You got me there. Hell, I was just making conversation. No harm in that, is there?"

"I believe that coffee's ready," said the other cowboy, speaking for the first time.

"I bet you're right about that," said Foss. "Help yourself to a cup."

The silent one took a ragged bandana out of his pocket. He used it to wrap around the hot handle of the coffeepot, and he poured himself a cupful. Then he sat back down. "Hell," said his partner, "pour them around."

"Oh," said the silent one. He set his own cup on the ground, got back up and poured three other cups full. Then he sat to drink his coffee. The other three men each picked up a cup. The talker took a tentative sip.

"Damn," he said. "That's hot. It's good, though. Good coffee. This is right neighborly of you. By the way, my name's Red Bandy. My talkative partner here is Candy Watson. What might be your handles?"

"Amos Foss," said the ex-lawman.

"Amos Foss?" said Bandy. "Seems like there was a lawman back at Whizbang by that name?"

"There was," said Foss. "He got himself fired."

Bandy laughed. "Was that you then?" he asked.

"That was me," said Foss.

"Well, I be damned," Bandy said. "You hear that, Candy? We're having coffee here with ol' Amos Foss, the badass lawman from Whizbang. But he went and got himself fired. Well, who they got for the law now that you ain't it no more?"

"I don't know," Foss said. "They hadn't yet made that decision by the time I left town."

"Well, well," Bandy said. "Amos Foss. That's pretty damn good, I'd say." Then he looked over at Slocum. "I didn't catch your name," he said.

"I never said it," said Slocum.

"Yeah," said Bandy. "Well, do you mind? What is it?"

"Slocum," Slocum said.

"Seems like I heard a that name, too," said Candy Watson. "Back in a place called Dead Dog. Another place called Drownding Creek. This Slocum killed some men. They said he was fast."

"Seems like I heard of them places, too," Slocum said.

The two cowboys looked at one another. They seemed suddenly a bit subdued, a little less certain of themselves. Red Bandy finished his coffee, put the cup on the ground and stood up. "Well," he said, "I think me and Candy here best be moving on. We sure thank you for the coffee."

Candy took a final slurp out of his cup and set it aside. He stood up to follow his leader.

"Which way you say you was headed?" Slocum asked.

"West," said Bandy.

"I don't think so," Slocum said.

Foss tensed for action.

"What do you mean?" asked Bandy.

"I don't want you riding west," said Slocum. "Is that clear enough?"

"Hell," Bandy said, "it's a free country, ain't it? This here is open range. We got to go where the horses is at, don't we?"

"That's what I'm afraid of," said Slocum. "We got some friends out there on a little horse ranch, and those four horses you're driving are shod and branded. You ain't hunting wild horses. You're hunting horses to steal."

"Now wait a minute," Bandy said.

"You said you wanted to use this campsite," Slocum said. "Use it. We'll take your horses and your guns. We'll leave you plenty of supplies—food and coffee. When we get back in a few days, we'll give you back your horses and guns, and you can go on your way."

"You crazy?" Bandy asked. "We ain't going for that."

"It's better than dying," Slocum said.

"I'd go crazy sitting around this place for more than a day," Watson said.

"I don't want to kill you," said Slocum. "I'm making you a good offer. It won't cost you but a few days, and you'll still be alive. What do you say?"

The two cowboys looked at one another but made no answer. Slocum thought about the men he was planning to kill. Three men. Maybe six. He didn't really want to add these two to the list. But he couldn't take a chance on having them run across Halley and Millicent on the ranch alone and steal Halley's horses, maybe do harm to the women.

"Tell you what," he said. "You give me your guns and your horses, wait here a few days, and I'll throw in a hundred dollars."

Both cowboys' jaws dropped.

"A hundred dollars?" said Bandy. "You serious?"

"I'm serious," said Slocum. "I told you I don't want you riding west. Not just yet anyhow. Well, what do you say?"

"Can we see the money?" Watson asked.

Slocum pulled some bills out of his pocket and counted out one hundred dollars. He tossed it on the ground in front of the two cowboys.

"I'll leave it here with you," he said. "Just a few days."

"That's good pay, boys," Foss said.

Bandy unbuckled his gun belt and let it drop to the ground.

"Go on, Candy," he said.

Watson did the same, and Slocum motioned them to move away from the guns. He picked them up, and Bandy picked up the money.

"You got a deal," Bandy said, thumbing through the bills. "Just a few days. Right? See you here in a few days."

Slocum and Foss rode along side by side and behind them trailed six horses. "We going to nursemaid all these horses all the way into Whizbang?" Foss asked.

"They might come in handy," Slocum said. "You never know."

"When we get done," said Foss, "you mean to take the horses and guns back to those boys?"

"That's what I said," Slocum answered.

"You know," said Foss, "I can't figure you. Back there, I was sure we were going to kill those two. Why didn't you?"

"Why didn't you?" Slocum said.

"I was waiting for you to make a move," said Foss, "or for one of them to make a play. It just never happened. That's all. Well, now, that's not all. You made sure it never happened. A hundred dollars! Hell, Slocum, that's a lot of money."

"You reckon two lives are worth a hundred dollars?" Slocum asked. "We don't know them two. We got them figured for horse thieves, and we're likely right about that, but if you still had your job, what would you do about them?"

"I'd arrest them, of course," Foss said.

"And then?" said Slocum.

"Well, they'd be charged with horse stealing," Foss said, "and then there'd be a trial to determine whether they were guilty or innocent."

"If we'd have killed them out there," Slocum said, "there wouldn't have been no trial. And you know, Foss, they might actually have bought them horses. We really don't know."

15

Millicent wasn't much help with the actual outdoor ranch work, so she threw herself into the housework. She cleaned the breakfast dishes, then went on cleaning. Toward noon, she started lunch. When Halley came back to the house after half a day's work, about the same time that Slocum and Foss stopped to make their noon camp, she found a meal waiting for her. She wolfed it down like any ranch hand, and she drank several cups of coffee. Neither she nor Millicent said much during the meal, but when they were done and they were sitting quietly across the table from one another over coffee, Halley said, "That was real nice, Millie. Thanks."

"Oh," Millicent said, "it's the least I can do. You've been so good to us—to me and Amos."

"The house looks real nice, too," Halley said. "Hell, it ain't looked this good in years. I guess I just ain't much for the housework."

"No one could expect you to be," Millicent said, "working this ranch the way you do. You must be worn out at the end of a day."

"Aw, it ain't so bad," Halley said. "To tell you the truth, I wouldn't have my life no other way. You know, ol' Slocum, he's prob'ly worrying right now about how he's fixing to break my heart when he rides on out of here for good. Don't tell him I said this, but he won't."

"Won't ride out?" Millicent said.

"He'll ride out, all right," said Halley. "It's in his blood. What he won't do is break my heart. I don't want to be tied to no one man like that. I like my freedom. I'm my own boss. I don't have no man telling me what to do every move I make, and I like it that way. And Slocum, well, that's what I like about him. We been having us a good time together, and he's been a big help around the place. But I know he'll move on sooner or later, and that's one of the reasons I like him so much. That make any sense to you?"

Millicent laughed a little. "No," she said. "It doesn't. Not really. But then, I don't believe I've ever met a woman quite like you."

Halley guffawed. "And likely never will again," she said. "Hell, I reckon when the good Lord seen what come out of the mold, he smashed the damn thing to bits." She laughed some more, and then she brought her hand down hard on the tabletop as if she were smashing something. "I don't want no more like that running around," she said. Millicent joined in her laughter. Soon they were quiet again, sipping coffee.

"Halley," Millicent said, "will they be all right?"

"Honey, if I was to worry about someone," Halley said, "I'd worry about them six men back there in Whizbang that's waiting to be killed but don't even know they're waiting. They'll come back." She paused a moment and took another sip of coffee. "Can I ask you a question?" she said.

"Of course," Millicent said.

"It ain't none of my business," said Halley.

"That's all right," Millicent said.

"What are you and Amos going to do when this is all over?" Halley asked.

Millicent rested an elbow on the table, her chin in the palm of her hand. "I don't know," she said. "Amos doesn't have a job anymore. I guess we'll just move on until he finds one. There's probably someone somewhere looking for a good lawman."

"Is that what you want?" Halley asked. "To sit home and wait for a lawman to get back, hope he made it through another day?"

"I haven't thought about it that much," Millicent said. "If it's what Amos wants, or if it's the only kind of work he can find, then I guess I'll just have to live with it."

"Let me give you something to think about," Halley said. "I don't know if either one of you'd be interested or not. I could use help around this place. If you and Amos was of a mind, we could work up some sort of partnering arrangement. It wouldn't be like you was hired hands. I guess I'd have a bigger share, 'cause I own the place outright. The place and the critters I have on it right now. But if y'all was to be interested, we could work something out."

"Why, I—I don't know what to say," Millicent stammered.

"Don't say nothing right now," said Halley. She picked up her cup and drank the last drops, then put it down and stood up. "When Amos gets back, talk it over with him. See how he feels about it. Then let me know. Well, time's a wasting. I best be getting at it again. See you later."

Halley put her hat back on and left the house, leaving Millicent sitting dumbfounded alone at the table.

Foss and Slocum rode the rest of that first day without incident. They made small talk now and then, but they did not talk about their mission, about the men they would face when they reached their destination. That evening they made another camp and ate another meal, still some of the food Halley had sent along with them. It would be their last good meal. The rest was standard trail food: tins of beans, hardtack. But they had plenty of coffee. They had left the pot and some coffee with the cowboys back at the noon campsite, but they still had some coffee, and they had a pot to boil it in. They ate and drank coffee, then settled back to smoke. Both of them were thinking of the job to be done when they reached Whizbang about this same time the next night.

But Amos Foss had other things on his mind, too. He had agreed to marry Millicent, and he did want to. It wasn't as if she had tricked him into it or anything like that. He did want her. Why, she was such a lovely lady in his mind that he had waited a long time before daring to speak to her about such matters, and to find out that she wanted him, too, well, it was just wonderful. He could scarcely believe his good fortune.

But Amos Foss had been brought up to believe that a man should be in good financial shape before he took a wife. That is to say, he should be well able to provide for her and to take care of her in a decent fashion. And Amos Foss had just lost his job. By himself, he could manage. But he hated to think of dragging Millicent around the country from town to town looking for work. And the only kind of work he could do was the work of a lawman.

Oh, he had worked on ranches as a young man. He could do that work all right, but a cowhand's wages would not support a man and a wife. He wanted Millicent to have a nice house, a place where she would be comfortable and secure, a home she would be proud of. He wondered how far he would have to ride, taking her along with him, before he could find a suitable job. It was eating at his mind. He decided that he'd better try to stop it, at least temporarily, if he didn't want it interfering with the job at hand.

"Slocum," he said, trying to think of something else, "you reckon those cowboys we left back there are doing all right?"

"They're likely trying to figure out how to divide up a hundred dollars by two," Slocum said. "Probably fighting with each other by now."

Foss chuckled. "I like the way you handled that situation back there, Slocum," he said. "I really do."

"Well," Slocum said, "just wait till tomorrow night. Things'll be a whole lot different then. There won't be no going easy on them."

"I know," said Foss. "You don't think we should try to take them alive?"

"Them three new ones," Slocum said, "you can do what you want about them as long as it don't interfere with my plans. I'm going to kill Cain and Barber and Hedley. That's all there is to it, Foss. Don't try to change my mind, and don't get in my way."

"Oh, hell, Slocum, I won't get in your way," Foss said, "and I'm not trying to change your mind. I just asked a question. That's all. I'm not carrying a badge anymore, and that makes a difference in my attitude. Especially considering the way the badge was taken away from me. I believe in the law. I really do. But the criminals back in Whizbang are also the town's lawmakers. That doesn't leave us much choice, the way I see it. When you first told me your story, I didn't know what I know now."

"I reckon not," Slocum said. "And I reckon I can't really blame you none for the way you handled things. All you had was just my word, and you didn't know me. Besides, I hadn't really seen what happened. I had just figured it out, and I didn't have no proof. No, I don't blame you none."

"I'm glad of that," Foss said. "Slocum?"

"Yeah?"

"If anything happens to me in Whizbang, will you see that Millicent is taken care of?"

"I promise you that," Slocum said.

"Thanks," said Foss. "Well, I guess I'll turn in. Long day tomorrow."

"Could still be a few long days ahead of us right now," Slocum said.

And the next day was indeed a long one. The rest of their ride to Whizbang was uneventful. They met no one else along the way. They stopped a few times to rest and water the horses, and they stopped about noon to eat. The rest of the day went about the same as the morning. They did not talk much. There wasn't much to say that they hadn't already gone over. It was a hot day with the sun overhead, and they were grateful for the evening at the end of their day of traveling.

They camped in the grove near where Harley had been killed. It was a safe distance away from Whizbang, and they would not likely be spotted. As soon as they got the camp set up, the horses all taken care of, and had eaten themselves a meal, Slocum checked his guns. He looked at Foss, and said, "Well, let's get to thinning out the herd."

"Already?" Foss asked.

"Why wait?" was Slocum's answer. "Let's go after one of your extra three and get him out of the way. You say which one."

"Hell, Slocum," Foss said, "I'm not the marshal anymore. I got no jail to lock someone up in. I hate to go to a man's house when he's got a wife and kids and take a chance on having to gun him down maybe right in front of them."

"All right," Slocum said. "I'll go along. So let's pick one out and watch. He won't be in the house with his wife and kids forever. We can get him when he's on his way to town—sometime when he goes out alone."

"Well then," Foss said, "the closest one to us is Alf Badger. He's got a wife, but they don't have any kids."

"Lead the way," said Slocum.

It wasn't long before they were looking down on a lone house not far outside of town. They dismounted and secured their horses. Slocum studied the situation. There was a small house, an outhouse, a small horse barn, and no other outbuildings. The spread was not a working ranch, not even a farm. It was just a home outside of town.

"What do you say?" Foss asked. "We just sit here and watch?"

"Let's go in and take a closer look," said Slocum.

They walked down the hillside and made their way in the darkness over close to the house. Slocum checked the barn and found two horses inside. Motioning Foss to follow him, he sneaked over to the house to look through a lighted window. He saw Badger sitting at the table, a sullen look on his face. Mrs. Badger was serving him a glass of whiskey. Her right eye was black and swollen, and the right side of her face was one big bruise. Her hair was a mess, and her dress was torn across the front.

Slocum pointed and Foss took a look.

"The worthless son of a bitch," he whispered. "I always suspected that, but there was never anything I could do."

"Well," said Slocum, "let's do something about it right now. Come on."

He led the way around to the front door and pulled out his Colt. Using the butt, he banged on the door. Then he stepped to one side. Foss stood on the other side. He pulled out his revolver.

"Alf," Foss called out. "It's Amos Foss. Come on out. I want to talk to you."

"What about?" came Badger's voice from inside the house. "I thought you'd left the country."

"Come on out and we'll talk," Foss called.

"You ain't got no authority around here no more," Badger yelled. "Get off my property."

"I'm his authority," Slocum said. "Now get your ass out here you lousy woman-beating son of a bitch."

"Who's that?" asked Badger. "Is that Slocum?"

"Get your ass out here and you'll find out," Slocum said.

"Come on out peaceable, Alf," Foss said, "and we won't shoot. I promise you that."

Inside the house, Alf Badger ran to a corner and picked up a shotgun. He pointed it at the door. "You come on in," he said. "I'm a skeered to go out there. Come on in. The door ain't locked."

"Watch out," screamed Mrs. Badger.

Outside, Slocum reached for the door. He shoved it inward and quickly stepped aside again. Badger's shotgun roared. Slocum gave a front window a backhand slap with his gunhand, straightening his arm with the Colt inside the house as the glass shattered. He fired a quick shot, and the slug slammed into Badger's chest.

"Uh, uh," Badger said, looking down foolishly at the seeping, fresh hole. He wobbled a bit. He relaxed and dropped his shotgun to the floor. Just as it clattered, his knees buckled and he dropped to them. His body swayed back and forth, then back again. His eyes glazed over and he crumpled into a lifeless lump. Mrs. Badger dropped heavily into a chair. Holstering his revolver, Foss hurried to her side.

"I'm sorry, Amy," he said. "He didn't give us a choice."

"It's a blessing," said Mrs. Badger.

"What?" Foss asked.

"Did he hit you?" asked Slocum. "Did he do that to you?"

"He beat the hell out of me," she said. She looked at the body on the floor. "It's a blessing," she repeated.

"Yes, ma'am," said Slocum. "I reckon it is."

"Are you all right?" Foss asked. "Do you need to see a doctor?"

"I'll be all right," she said.

"What about money?" asked Foss. "Will you make it all right on your own?"

"I reckon what was his is mine," she said. "He had some cash here at the house and more in the bank. I reckon it's mine now."

"You're right about that," said Foss. "If the bank gives you any problems, you let us know."

"Yeah," she said. "Thanks. You know what? I hate to stay out here by myself. I'd like to go get me a room in town. Do you suppose?—"

"You change your clothes," said Foss. "Gather up anything from here that you'll need. We'll wait outside till you're ready. Then we'll take you to town."

Slocum walked back to the small barn and hitched one of the horses there to a small buggy that stood just outside. He drove the buggy to the front of the house. He got out and went back to the barn for the other horse. He put a bridle on it as if for riding, but he led it around to the front of the house bareback. In another few minutes, Mrs. Badger came outside. Foss took the bundle she carried and put in in the buggy.

"Go ahead and drive her in," Slocum said. "I'll be along with your horse."

Foss wondered what Slocum was up to, but he kept it to himself. He helped Mrs. Badger into the buggy, then climbed in after her and took up the reins. The buggy headed for town with a lurch. Slocum watched for a moment, then went back into the house. He dragged the body of Alf Badger out and loaded it onto the bareback horse. He gathered the horse's reins along with those of Foss's mount, climbed onto the back of his Appaloosa, and rode after the buggy.

By the time they delivered Mrs. Badger to a rooming house and tied the horse with Badger's body slung across its back to the rail in front of the ashes where the marshal's office used to be, it was getting late. They were lucky that they had managed all that without being seen in town, and Slocum suggested that they get out while they could. They headed for the campsite by the stream. Riding along, Foss said, "They'll all know we're back come morning. Do you think that's a good idea? There's still five of them, you know."

"Good idea or bad," Slocum said, "it's done. We couldn't hardly leave that woman out there alone, and she might need to show her old man's body in order to claim his money at the bank. From just the little I seen, I'd say that woman has had a rough enough life without us adding any to it."

"Well," said Foss, "I have to agree with you on that. What's our next step?"

"We settle in at our camp for the night," said Slocum. "In the morning, you tell me who's next on the list."

They were up early the next morning, and they had their breakfast and coffee. Most of the town folks wouldn't even be moving around yet. When they finished their coffee and cleaned up their mess, Slocum asked, "All right, Foss, who's our next easiest target?"

"Murf Richie lives on the west edge of town," Foss said. "He's got a wife and two kids, but he works in town. He'll be headed in, likely alone, around seven-thirty or so. He's a man of habit, and he's punctual."

"Lead the way," said Slocum.

16

"I'm going up in my north pasture to hunt for strays," Halley said. "I won't make it back by noon, so don't fix me nothing."

Millicent straightened up quickly. "Do you mind if I ride along?" she asked. "I might not be much help, but I promise not to get in the way or hold you up. I can ride."

"Well—well, hell no," Halley said. "I don't mind. Company'll be nice for a change. Get dressed for it, and I'll saddle us a couple of horses."

"I'll meet you out at the corral," Millicent said.

In a few minutes, they were mounted and riding.

"You didn't lie," Halley said. "You do set a horse well."

"Thank you," Millicent said. "It's real pleasant. Before Amos brought me out here, I was cooped up in that kitchen in Whizbang for a whole year."

"I don't know how you stood it so long," Halley said. "It woulda made me crazy as a cow in loco weed."

"I don't know either how I managed," said Millicent. "I did, though, and I guess that's what matters—that and the fact that I'm out of there now, and I have Amos."

"Amos Foss is a good man, Millie," Halley said. "You hang onto him. And when them two gets back, you tell Amos about my offer. It ain't no handout neither. I can

148

use the help and the company. If you two take me up on it, we'll build another house for you so we won't all be crowded into my little ranch house. New marrieds needs their privacy anyhow."

Millicent blushed a little. "I'll tell him," she said. "It's awfully good of you. I hope he says yes. I think I'd like to stay here."

Watson drank the last of a cup of coffee and pitched the tin cup on the ground. "Damn it," he said, "I'd sure like a glass of whiskey."

"A cold beer wouldn't be so bad," said Bandy.

"A cold beer would be good," Watson agreed. "I'm sure as hell getting bored with nothing but branch water and coffee."

"Beans," said Bandy.

"We ought to have killed them two and went on to town," Watson said.

"We could have tried," said Bandy. "You do recollect who them two is, don't you?"

"Yeah," said Watson. "I know."

"We tried to take them on," Bandy said, "we wouldn't be setting here bored, that's for sure. We'd be dead."

"I know," said Watson, kicking a rock.

"And what's more, even if we hadn't a run across them old boys," Bandy said, "if we had just rode on hunting up more horses, we'd of worked our ass off for a few more days, still had no whiskey nor beer, and when it was over and done, we wouldn't have as much money as what Slocum give us to just set here. So I suggest you quit your bellyaching and try to have a little patience."

"Red?" said Watson.

"Yeah?"

"Red, I been a thinking."

"Now, that there's a dangerous thing for you to be doing," said Bandy.

"Damn it, Red," said Watson, "I'm serious."

"All right, Candy," said Bandy. "Hell, I'm just joshing you. What you been thinking about anyhow?"

"I been thinking that maybe we hadn't ought to have stole them horses," Watson said. "You know?"

"Hell," said Bandy, "we didn't have no money. We couldn't find no jobs. What the hell was we supposed to do? Starve our young asses to death?"

"No," said Watson. "Hell, I don't know. But maybe we should have just kept looking for work. You know, looked a little harder. That's all."

"You thinking that ex-lawman might tell on us?" Bandy said. "Get our asses throwed in jail?"

"No," Watson said. "I don't think he'll do that. Them two was pretty fair with us."

Bandy stared at the ground between his feet. "They was," he said. "And I reckon you're right."

" 'Bout what?" Watson asked.

"We hadn't ought to have stole them horses," Bandy said.

Watson picked up the coffeepot and looked over at Bandy. "You want another cup of coffee?" he asked.

Murf Richie was riding the short trail from his house to town, when he saw Amos Foss standing in the middle of the trail blocking his way. Foss held a rifle in his hands. Richie felt a moment of panic and thought about trying to ride Foss down. He changed his mind quickly, though, and he stopped his horse.

"Amos," he said. "What are you doing here?"

"I came back to clean up a mess," said Foss, "and you're a part of it. You got a wife and kids, Murf. I don't want to kill you."

"What do you want?" Richie said.

"I want you to surrender to me," said Foss. "I'll take you to the nearest law and file charges against you. You'll get a trial."

"I didn't do nothing," said Richie. His horse nickered and fidgeted sideways, and he fought to control it. "I never killed no one. I never even shot no one."

"You were there," Foss said. "You were part of the conspiracy. What's it going to be?"

"I ain't no gunfighter," said Richie. "Even if I was, you're already holding that rifle ready. I don't want to get killed when I didn't do nothing."

"Then pull that revolver out real careful," Foss said, "and drop it on the ground."

Richie took hold of the butt of his revolver with his thumb and index finger and slowly withdrew it from the holster. He held it out away from himself at arm's length, then let go. It thudded to the ground.

"Now climb down out of the saddle," Foss said, "and put your hands behind your back."

Richie did as Foss told him to do, and just then Slocum stepped onto the road. Richie was astonished.

"You was there all along," he said. "If I'd a tried to fight Amos—"

"I'd have stayed out of it," Slocum said, "but if you'd have killed him, which I doubt, you'd have had to face me next. Then I'd have killed you for sure."

Slocum took a short piece of rope, which he'd been carrying in his left hand, and wrapped it around both of Richie's wrists. He tied a good tight knot, securing Richie's hands behind his back.

"Now you can get back on your horse," Slocum said, and he gave Richie a hand up. He walked off the road again and came back in a couple of minutes with his and Foss's horses. They mounted up and rode away, leading Richie along behind them.

Gordon Slick stood in front of the ruins of the marshal's office staring at the body of Alf Badger dangling there across the bare back of a horse. His eyes were wide. He licked his lips and looked around nervously. Then he noticed Sammy Cain hurrying his way. He stood there until Cain reached him. "Look," he said, pointing at the body on the horse. "Look at that. It's Alf. He's killed. Killed and brought in to us."

"That ain't all," Cain said.

"What do you mean?" asked Slick.

"Murf Richie ain't showed up in town," Cain said. "No one's seen him."

"Has anyone rode out to his house?" Slick asked.

"No one that I know of," Cain admitted.

"Well, ride on out there," said Slick. "Maybe he ain't feeling good, or maybe he just slept late. Maybe there ain't nothing wrong."

"I ain't riding out there," Cain said. "Maybe something is wrong, like with Alf here. I ain't riding out there and let them get hold of me and do me thataway."

"Who do you think 'them' is?" Slick asked.

"Slocum," said Cain, "and Amos. That's what I think. I think Slocum lived, and I think somehow Amos got out there and found him. That's what I think. And I think they've came back here to kill us all. That's what I think. And I ain't riding out to Murf's place neither. If you want to find out bad enough, you ride on out there your own self."

"All right. All right," Slick said. "Then go find Chunk and Doby and tell them to get their guns and get their ass on over to the Booze Palace. I'll meet y'all there. While you're at it, find someone to haul ol' Alf's carcass on out of here."

They met there in the back room of the saloon, Slick wearing pinned on his vest the badge they had demanded back from Amos Foss. All four were heavily armed. All faces were tense. Slick nervously licked dry lips. He hefted the revolver at his side as if he wanted to use it on someone. Finally he spoke.

"You three bastards are the only ones left what killed that cowboy," he said. "I figured this whole thing out now. That Slocum, he wants to kill you three. That's all he wants."

"Wait just a minute, Gordie," said Chunk Hedley. "Amos is with him now, and it was you that shot Amos. Don't think you can write yourself out of this mess we're in."

"I wasn't trying to do that," Slick said. "I was just think-ing it through. That's all."

"Well, stop thinking on them lines," Hedley said. "We know it's Slocum and Amos Foss out there, and we know that between the two of them, they mean to get all of us. Now we got to figure out what to do about it."

"Yeah. Yeah. I know," said Slick. "Listen. They got Alf and Murf 'cause they slipped up on them and caught them by surprise. None of us thought we'd ever see either one of them two again, so they was able to sneak up. Well, they can't do that again. We know they're back now. We'll be ready for them."

"Has anyone seen them?" asked Doby Barber.

"What?" Slick said.

"Has anyone seen them?" Barber repeated. "Seen either one of them?"

"Well, no," said Slick, "but—"

"Then we don't even know it's really them," Barber said. "Alf was a mean son of a bitch. Anyone could a killed him. Hell, maybe even his missus. A woman can shoot a gun, you know. She's over to the boarding house right now. Maybe she shot him. And ain't no one seen Murf, dead or alive. Maybe he ain't even killed. Maybe we're getting all excited here over nothing."

"Goddamn it, Doby," Hedley said, "Alf's dead. That ain't no maybe."

"Wait a minute," said Slick. "Wait a minute. Doby just might have something there. You say the missus is over to the boarding house?"

"That's right," said Barber. "She looks like ol' Alf had slapped her around some again, too. Maybe she shot him for that. Maybe she got tired of it and shot him."

"Come along with me," said Slick. "We'll just have a little talk with her."

They banged on the door but got no answer. They banged again, and Slick yelled through the door. "Mizz Badger. This is Marshal Slick. Now we know you're in there, and we need to have a little talk. Open up the door and let us in."

In another moment, the door was opened, and Mrs. Badger, her head ducked as if to hide the bruises on her face, stepped aside to let them in. She moved to the far side of the room. Slick went in first and the others followed. For a brief while, no one spoke. Slick took off his hat and held it in both hands in front of himself.

"Mizz Badger," he said, "we found your husband's body over at the marshal's office, well, where the office used to be, this morning. He was slung over a horse. Someone brought him in and left him there for us to find. Do you know anything about that?"

"It must have been that other man that done that," she said.

"What other man?" said Slick.

"It was two of them," she said. "Amos Foss and another man. I don't recall his name. Maybe I heard it. I don't recall."

"Was it Slocum?" asked Sammy Cain.

"It might have been," she said. "I can't be sure."

"Tell us what happened, Miz Badger," Slick said.

"They knocked on the door late last night," she said. "Amos Foss called out for Alfie to open up the door and come outside. Alfie got his shotgun and blasted away at them through the door. Then one of them shot him through the window. They come on in then to see if I was all right, and then Amos Foss offered to bring me into town. He brung me in the buggy. I don't know what the other man done. Maybe it was him brought Alfie in. I don't know."

"This other man," Slick said, "what did he look like?"

"I wouldn't know how to describe him exactly," she said. "I guess kind of average. I don't know."

"Did you see his horse?" Slick asked.

"It was a big one," she said. "Had spots on his rump."

"Appaloosa," said Hedley.

"It was Slocum," Cain said.

"Well, thank you, Miz Badger," said Slick. "Sorry to have to bother you in your time of grief."

"Ain't no grief," she said. "Alfie was no damn good. He'd just beat me up when they come. I'm glad they done it, and I'm a witness. I'll say it was self-defense. Alfie shot at them first. With a shotgun. He deserved what he got. He was a no-good yellow dog. That's what he was. A no-good yellow dog."

"Well," Slick said, "we'll be running on now. Thank you, ma'am."

Back out in the street, the four men stopped. They looked up and down the street and up toward the former site of Slocum's camp that had overlooked Whizbang. "If I ever have me a wife," said Sammy Cain, "and if I was to get myself killed, I sure hope she wouldn't be talking about me like that."

"I don't think you have to worry none about that, Sammy," Hedley said. "Ain't no woman would have you. Besides, we're all like to get killed before any of us would have time to find us a wife."

"Shut up," said Slick. "I don't want to hear that kind of talk."

"All right," Barber said, "but what're we going to do? It was Amos and that Slocum, weren't it? Almost for sure?"

"It was them all right," Slick said. "They've come back for us."

"What about ol' Murf?" Cain asked.

"They got him, too," said Slick.

"But we ain't seen no body," said Hedley. "They killed Alf, and they brung the body in for us to see. If they'd killed Murf, wouldn't they a done the same thing?"

"I can't read their goddamned minds," Slick said, "but they got him all right. He ain't been seen, has he? They got him. Come on. Let's go back over to the Palace."

Slocum and Foss made Richie take off his boots, and they tied him to a tree at their new campsite by the stream. They searched him, making sure that he had no knife to use in cutting the ropes. Unless someone happened along, there was no way he would get loose. Even someone passing by on the nearby road wouldn't see him through the trees.

"And if you do find a way to get loose," Slocum said, "I'll come after you, and I won't be as nice as Foss here was. I'll just kill you."

"I ain't going nowhere," said Richie. "I'll take my chances with the law."

Slocum walked over to Foss. "We got four left," he said. "That one that shot you, and three of the mob that killed Harley: there's Barber, Cain, and Hedley. My guess is they're all bunched up by now."

"Likely in the Booze Palace," Richie volunteered. Slocum and Foss turned to look at him.

"Why do you say that?" Slocum asked.

"Ol' Gordie had hisself named marshal," Richie said. "Since the marshal's office burned down, he just hangs out at the Palace. It's his favorite place anyhow. They can put someone upstairs and watch pretty good in all directions, and they've likely stashed plenty of guns and bullets in there, too. It's just a guess, but I'd bet on it. That's where they'll be."

Slocum looked back at Foss. "The Booze Palace," he said. "What do you think?"

"It makes sense," said Foss. "Like Murf says—it could make a pretty good fortress. So Gordon Slick's got my job, has he? The little shit."

"He won't have it for long," said Slocum.

"Yeah," Foss said. "We going anyplace right away?"

Slocum shook his head. "Not right away," he said.

"Want me to make some coffee?" Foss asked.

"Sounds good," Slocum said. He paced away and back. "How can we get at them in that damn saloon?" he asked.

"We can't get at them in there," Foss said, picking up the pot and walking toward the water. "Not without being seen somewhere along the way. We could maybe sneak in on it at night. Maybe."

He knelt at the water's edge to fill the pot. Then he stood up and headed back toward the small campfire. Slocum pulled a bag of coffee grounds out of a saddlebag and handed it to Foss as he walked by. Foss took it and moved on to the fire. He dumped some grounds into the pot of water, then knelt down to set the coffee on the fire.

"Can we get to it from the back of the building?" Slocum asked.

"I don't think so," Foss said. "It's pretty clear back there, too. If they have anyone watching, we'll be spotted for sure. They'd have a good clean rifle shot at us, too."

"Well then, by God," said Slocum, "we'll just have to think of something else. That's all."

17

When the people of Whizbang began to stir the next morning, they saw the old camp of Slocum set up anew just on the other side of the town limits sign. They could see that there were three men up there sitting around a campfire. They gathered in small groups and looked and pointed and speculated about what it meant. Most of the citizens of the town knew little about the causes of the recent violence in their midst. Some thought that Slocum must be some kind of evil gunfighter intent on the destruction of their town. Others, having got wind of Amos Foss's association with Slocum, feared something deeper than that. Most were just confused and curious.

Eventually Slick, Cain, Barber, and Hedley formed their own little group. For a moment they stared up at the camp in silence. Finally Barber spoke up and said, "They's three men, but they's a bunch of horses."

"What do you make of that, Slick?" Cain asked.

"I don't know," said Slick. He was staring at the camp, squinting because of the bright early morning sky. "I'd say Slocum and Amos Foss. Looks like they got them some help though. They's a third man up there."

"They's a bunch of horses," said Barber.

"That could mean more men," Slick said.

"Where are they then?" asked Hedley.

"Hell," said Cain, "we don't know who they are. They could be anywhere. They could be down here amongst us."

Hedley looked around nervously. "I don't see no strangers in town," he said.

"They could be anywhere," said Cain.

"I wonder who that third man up there is," Slick mused.

"Hey," said Barber, "I got an old spyglass over in my shop."

"Well, run and get the son of a bitch," Slick said.

Barber hurried off. The other three kept staring at the little camp. "How many horses is up there?" Hedley asked. "How many would you say?"

"I can see eight," Cain said. "That goddamn big spotty-ass horse and seven more. That's all I can see."

"Then there could be eight men up there," Hedley said.

"They's three up there for sure," said Cain. "Maybe five more laying around that we can't see. Maybe five more anywhere."

"They wouldn't be too far away without their horses," Hedley said. "Would they?"

"They could be down here in town," said Slick.

"I don't see them," Hedley said. "I don't see no strangers."

"I think we done had this conversation," said Slick. "It sure ain't going nowhere."

Barber came panting back with his spyglass, and Slick yanked it away from him. He pointed the glass at the camp and stuck its small end to his left eye. Squinting his right eye, he made some adjustments to the spyglass.

"I see Slocum," he said. "Son of a bitch is smoking a cee-gar as calm as you please. There's Amos. Goddamn. That there's Murf with them. Murf Richie."

"The double-crossing son of a bitch," said Cain, reaching for the spyglass. "Let me see that thing."

"I don't know about that," said Slick, ignoring Cain's request. "Looks to me like he might be tied up. It's kind of hard to tell for sure. It's Murf though. I see him plain as day."

"Do you see anyone else?" Hedley asked.

"No one else," said Slick. "Just them three. Them three and eight horses."

By the time the sun was high overhead, some of the people in town had gone on about their business, but a few clusters still stood around staring at the camp. One of the clusters was that of Slick, Cain, Barber, and Hedley. The three men in the camp above watched them.

"How long are you two going to just set here like this?" Richie asked them.

"It ain't nothing for you to worry about," Slocum said.

"Long as it takes, I reckon," said Foss.

"I'm getting kinda hungry," Richie said.

"You'll get hungrier before it's over," Slocum said. He took a drag on his cigar, then laid it aside. He reached over and picked up his Winchester. He cranked a shell into the chamber, then raised the rifle to his shoulder. He took careful aim.

Back down in the street, Barber raised the spyglass to his eye, Slick having finally relinquished it. He was looking at Richie.

"I think he is tied up," he said. "Slocum and Amos caught him, and they've got him tied up. That's what. He never double-crossed us after all. He's their prisoner."

"Prisoners talk," said Cain.

"Could be," Slick agreed.

Barber moved the glass over to look at Amos Foss. Then he moved it on to focus on Slocum, and he saw the Winchester aimed straight at him. "Goddamn!" he shouted. "He's fixing to shoot." The group of four scattered in four directions just as the shot rang out. Dirt was kicked up in the street where Barber had been standing. Suddenly all the people standing in the street became animated. Others came running out of shops and out of houses to look.

Slocum put down the rifle and picked up his cigar. He took a couple of puffs to make sure it was still going.

"What'd you do that for?" Richie asked.

"Give them something more to worry about," said Slocum. "Say, we got anymore coffee in that pot?"

Halley came home for lunch, and Millicent already had a big spread laid out. The two ladies sat down and ate together. Then Halley poured them each another cup of coffee.

"That was mighty good, Millie," Halley said.

"Thank you," said Millicent, but she seemed somewhat distracted.

"What's wrong?" Halley asked her. "I can tell it's something."

"I'm worried about Amos and John," said Millicent. "I can hardly stand it. Halley will you loan me a horse and saddle?"

"You fixing to ride after them?" Halley asked.

"Yes," said Millicent. "I want to."

"Then let's both go," Halley said. "You pack us a bunch of food while I go out and saddle a couple of horses."

"Right now?" Millicent said, her face brightening up.

"Why wait?" Halley said, as she stood up and put her hat on. She headed for the door, and Millicent too jumped up from her chair.

"All right," she said.

Slick, Cain, Hedley, and Barber were gathered again inside the Booze Palace. They were not, however, sitting at their favorite corner table. Instead they were at the front of the big main room. Looking out the window there, they could watch the Slocum camp. Slick was standing at the window. The others sat at a nearby table. There was a whiskey bottle on the table, and the three seated men each had a glass. There was a fourth glass on the table for Slick.

"They ain't moved up there," Slick said.

"Anyone else showed up?" asked Hedley.

"Just them same three is all," Slick said.

"I'm sure curious about all them extra horses," Hedley said.

"Yeah," said Barber, standing up and taking his glass to move over by the window with Slick. "And the men what rode them. Where the hell are they?"

"The bastards are cooking a meal," Slick said. "They're going to sit up there and eat while we watch them."

"What are we going to do, Gordie?" Barber asked.

"Sammy," Slick said to Cain, "you're a pretty good rifle shot, ain't you?"

"I ain't bad," Cain said.

"Can you hit one of them from here?" Slick asked.

Cain stood up and moved to the window. "It's a long shot," he said. He walked to the door and positioned himself in the doorway as he would to shoot. "A hell of a long shot. If I was to make it, it'd be the best shot I ever made. It'd have to be a good shot, and it would have to be a lucky one, too."

"Where's your rifle?" Slick asked.

"Out on my horse," said Cain.

"Why don't you go get it and try a shot?" Slick said.

Cain stood in the doorway for a few quiet seconds, looking up at the camp in the distance. Then he hurried out to his horse at the rail, jerked out the rifle from the scabbard and hurried back in. He cranked a shell into the chamber. Then he braced himself against the doorway and raised the rifle to his shoulder. He took his time getting settled and sighting in.

"Give me that spyglass," Slick said, and Barber handed it over. Slick sighted in on the camp with the spyglass and watched. Cain squeezed the trigger, and the rifle roared and bucked. "Shit," said Slick, "you got Murf. You got him. Try another shot. Hurry it up."

Up at the campsite, Slocum and Foss each grabbed their rifles as Murf Richie fell forward into the fire. Both men fired as fast as they could into the front door and the front window of the Booze Palace down below.

As bullets thudded into the doorjamb and the walls around the door, Sammy Cain whooped and danced away, moving back into the room. At the same time, Slick and the others were showered with glass as bullets smashed the big front window. They yelled and scampered back into the safety of the center of the room as well.

"Damn you," said Dutch from behind the bar. "You started it now."

"Shut up," said Slick.

Other customers in the saloon got up hurriedly and left by the back door. No one was left in the place but the four conspirators and Dutch.

"Now what?" Cain said.

"Maybe we can slip up on them after dark," Slick said.

"Shit," said Cain. "You know they'll be expecting that. We'd walk right into a trap. That's what we'd be doing."

"They've stopped shooting," Barber said.

Slick eased his way back to the now-shattered front window to sneak a look. He found the spyglass on the floor and picked it up. Looking through it, he saw no sign of either Slocum or Foss. He saw Richie's corpse. Someone had dragged it out of the fire. The fire still burned. The eight horses were still there where they had been. He turned to reach for the whiskey bottle on the table, but it was shattered. He walked over to the bar and ordered another. Dutch gave it to him, and he drank from the bottle.

"Well?" said Barber. He got no answer. "Well, what'd you see?"

"No sign of Slocum or Foss," Slick said. "That's what I seen. No sign of either one of them."

"That got them spooked, all right," Foss said.

"I reckon," said Slocum. The two men had simply moved back a little from the campsite to hide behind some boulders. From their new vantage point, they were still able to keep their eyes on the street below.

"The question is," said Foss, "what will they do now that they're spooked?"

"I can't answer that one," Slocum said. "We'll just have to wait and see. We sure do need to keep watching that damn street down there, though. Watch it like a couple of hawks."

"Yeah," Foss agreed.

• • •

It was the morning of their second day of riding when Millicent and Halley came across the two cowboys at the camp that had originally been set up by Slocum and Foss. Halley pulled a rifle out of a scabbard, cranked a shell into the chamber, and then moved slowly toward the camp. Millicent followed her. When the two cowboys saw the two women approaching, they grinned and stood up to greet them.

"Well now," said Red Bandy, "what've we got here?"

"Nothing for you to get too excited about," Halley said.

"Well," Bandy said, "we was just getting a meal started here. How would you two ladies like to join us?"

"We might," said Halley, "but keep your distance."

She swung a leg over her saddle and dropped to the ground. Millicent, too, dismounted. Halley walked toward the cowboys, still holding the rifle ready.

"You—you don't need that gun on us," Bandy said. "We ain't going to do you no harm."

"I don't see no horses," Halley said. "Men without horses in this country's likely to do anything to get some."

"Aw, well," Bandy said, "we got horses, all right. It's just that some other fellas borried them for a few days. They'll be coming back with them. We ain't stranded out here but just for a few days."

"If you'll stay on that side of the fire," said Halley, "we'll stay on this side. We'll stop a spell and eat with you."

"All right," said Bandy. "That's all right."

He headed for the far side of the fire, and Candy Watson followed him. Their footsteps were mincing, and then Halley noticed that they were barefoot. She realized just then that she couldn't see any guns anywhere around the camp. The cowboys sat on the ground on the other side of the fire from the women. Then Halley, followed by Millicent, moved close to the fire. The women sat.

"Go on ahead, ladies," said Bandy. "Dish yourselves up some grub. Me and Candy here will wait our turn."

Millicent moved forward to fix plates for Halley and

herself. Both women kept close watch on the two cow-boys. When Millicent gave Halley her plate and then sat back down with her own, she gave the two cowboys a hard look.

"You two met up with John Slocum and Amos Foss, didn't you?" she said.

"What?" said Bandy.

"There's no need in lying to me about it," she said. "I prepared this food for them myself, and I recognize the dishes."

Halley raised the rifle. "Where are they?" she asked. "What have you done?"

Both cowboys raised their hands over their heads. "Now wait a minute," Bandy said. "We ain't done nothing. Don't shoot that thing."

"Ma'am, uh, ladies," said Watson, speaking for the first time since the women had come into the camp, "we did do something, too. This here was their camp. Slocum and Foss. You're right. We rode in, and they spotted us for horse thieves right away. Well, whenever we said that we was headed west to hunt more horses—we pretended we was hunting wild horses, you see—whenever we said we was headed west, Slocum, he said that he didn't want us headed west. He took our horses and our guns and our boots, and he left us some food and stuff and a hundred dollars. He said he'd bring our stuff back in a few days."

"That's the truth, ladies," Bandy said.

Halley burst out laughing.

"What's so funny?" Bandy asked.

"That's our Slocum," Halley said, when she managed to speak again. "That's your good fortune, too. He had a choice of either killing you or paying you to sit here, and you lucked out. That's all. And the reason he didn't want you two riding west and a stealing horses is because of my little horse ranch out thataway."

"I kinda figured that," said Bandy, ducking his head and looking ashamed.

"Ma'am," Watson said, "Mr. Foss and Mr. Slocum, they

kinda put a scare on us, and they kinda taught us a lesson, too. We've been setting here with nothing to do but think and talk, and I just want you to know that, even when we get our own horses and guns back, well, your horses are going to be safe."

"They'll be safe from us," Bandy said.

"That's what I mean, ma'am," Watson went on. "We ain't going to do no more stealing. We're looking for honest work from here on out. In fact, if they bring back those four horses we stole, we aim to take them back where they belong. I just wanted you to know that, ma'am."

"Well, boys," said Halley, "I'm glad you told us that, and I believe you."

She laid her rifle aside and picked up the plate of food that Millicent had brought her. She figured that if either of the cowboys meant to make a move against her, this would be his chance. She tried to act unconcerned, but she really kept herself alert for anything that might happen. Bandy made a sudden move and she tensed, ready for action. He picked up a plate and began to dish himself out a meal. She relaxed. She was glad that she hadn't made herself obvious in her readiness.

18

"I still think we'll be walking into a trap if we go up there," said Cain.

"Hell," said Slick, "we got to do something. If we move real careful and keep ourselves spread out, we'll be all right. We can get the bastards. Besides, they got to sleep sometime, don't they? I'm tired of sitting around here the way we been doing. What do you say?"

"Well," said Barber, "this bullshit has been making me crazy. Let's go get them."

"Okay," Hedley said. "I'm with you."

"Sammy?" Slick said, turning back to Cain.

"All right," said Cain. "Fuck it. Let's go do it."

They each checked their six guns. Slick had decided that rifles would just get in the way. They wouldn't be firing at great distances in the dark anyhow. Barber walked to the shattered front window of the Booze Palace.

"Is it dark enough yet?" he asked.

"Hell," said Slick, "it's blacker'n the ace of spades. It's as dark as it's going to get. Come on."

The four conspirators slipped out the back door of the saloon and made their way down the alley to the far end of town. Then they walked out to the outcropping of rocks in the distance. From there they went along the bottom of the outcropping until they had reached a spot some distance to the left of the two men in the camp above them. They started climbing toward the top. It wasn't a long climb, but it was steep in some places, and in the dark, it was a bit treacherous. Barber slipped and scraped his shin.

"Ow. Goddamn," he said.

"Hush it up," said Slick in a harsh whisper. "Keep quiet, damn it."

"That hurt," Barber said.

"I don't give a shit if you break your fucking leg," Slick said. "Next one makes any noise, I'll kill him. I mean it."

They continued climbing then until they finally reached the top. Slick turned to his left. He knew that Slocum and Foss were now somewhere directly in front of him. His cohorts lined up behind him. Impatiently, he motioned to them to spread out. Then he started moving in a direction calculated to bring them up behind the small camp.

They walked slowly, trying to stay quiet. The crunching of their footsteps in the otherwise quiet of the night sounded loud. Slick tried to control their movements and their pace with hand gestures, but the others could scarcely see him the darkness. They moved on. At last, Slick could see glowing embers ahead and slightly below. He held up a hand and waved it. Then he pointed. They moved even more cautiously ahead. Slick stopped. His heart pounded in his chest.

He could now make out two forms under blankets beside the fire. He could hardly believe his good fortune. Both men were sleeping. The fools, he thought. He grinned and pointed, hoping to attract the attention of the other three to his discovery. The others, not able to tell what his wild gestures were all about, moved in and clustered around him. Emboldened by the sight ahead, he whispered to them.

"Look," he said. "They're sleeping. Let's move in a little closer to be sure of our shots, and then let's fill them full. Empty your guns in the bastards."

He led the way, and soon they were close enough to be confident of their shots. The four men pulled out their six-guns and took aim. Three of them waited for Slick to make the first move. He fired. Then the others all started firing. It sounded like a small war. Twenty-four shots were fired in rapid succession before the night was again silent. There was a ringing in the air from the blasts, and the atmosphere was filled with the pungent odor of burnt gunpowder.

"We did it," Barber said. Then he shouted, "We did it!"

"Come on," said Slick. "Let's go down and check."

Just then a shot rang out and a bullet spanged on a rock just at Slick's feet. He hopped and fell back hard on his ass. "Yow!" he yelled. Another shot sounded, and Slick rolled hard to his left. He hadn't realized how close to the edge he was, so he rolled much farther than he had meant to. He bounced his way almost all the way back down to the base of the outcropping, yelping all the way.

Up above, another shot sounded. The other four men turned to run. Barber and Hedley ran smack into one another. "Damn it," Hedley said. "Get out of my way." They shoved at each other for a few seconds before they managed to extricate themselves from the tangle. Then Hedley started running, but he stopped. He was running toward the camp. "Shit," he said. He stopped and turned to run the other direction.

Barber, in his confusion, ran right over the edge and tumbled after Slick. He screamed all the way down. Cain had run west, toward nothing but empty space. He ran until he could run no more, and then he stopped and panted, trying to catch his breath. His chest heaved in pain, and his legs ached. At last he stood and looked around himself. He was alone in the middle of nowhere in the dark night. He turned and started walking back toward town, but he planned to walk the long way around the camp.

Hedley ran across the ridge of the outcropping until he found himself back approximately at the place where they had climbed up. He started down that way, slipped and slid a few feet, scraping his back and butt. "Ow. Ow," he cried. He stopped himself and started his descent again. A rock moved under his foot, and he felt himself flung forward. He rolled the rest of the way down the hill.

* * *

With the first sign of daylight, Slocum built up the fire. Foss prepared the coffeepot and set it on to boil. In a short time they were seated comfortably, having their morning coffee and looking down on the main street of Whizbang. There was no sign of life down there yet.

"It's a nice morning, Mr. Foss," said Slocum.

"The beginning of a beautiful day, Mr. Slocum," Foss said.

"Yes sir," Slocum said, "there ain't nothing quite like sitting at a campfire out in the open having your first coffee of a morning and watching the sun peek over the far horizon."

"Why, Mr. Slocum," said Foss, "you're a damned poet."

"Why, thank you, Mr. Foss," Slocum said. He tipped back his cup and emptied it. Then he leaned forward to pour himself a refill. Still holding the pot, he looked over at Foss. "How's yours?" he asked.

"I think I'll have a warm up, if you don't mind," Foss said. He held out his cup and Slocum poured it full. He put the pot back on the edge of the fire. Then he leaned back to relax again.

"We ought to check our weapons here in a little bit," Slocum said. "It might could turn out to be an exciting day."

"Yeah," said Foss. "That's a good idea. Those dummies in our beds last night was another of your good ideas."

"It did the trick, didn't it?" Slocum said. "Today's going to be the day to wind this thing up once and for all. Those old boys are spooked real bad now, and they're sore as hell. Likely stiff. They'll be moving slow, and ever' move they make is going to hurt."

"They won't be coming back up here," said Foss. "Do you mean to go down there and get them?"

"I reckon we'll have to do just that," Slocum said.

It was daylight before Sammy Cain made his way back into Whizbang. He hobbled to the back door of the Booze palace and let himself in. There were the other three sitting at a table in the middle of the room. Slick had chosen the table as a good compromise. His favorite table was too far from the window. They couldn't look out at Slocum's camp. The table by the window was too close, too exposed. So he took a central table, halfway between. Dutch was nowhere around. It was too early in the morning for saloon business. Even so, the conspirators drank whiskey. Their experience of the night before demanded it.

"Goddamn it," said Cain as he walked in to join the gathering, "I told you it would be a trap. I knew it all along. Shit. I been walking the whole damn night."

"Shut up and have a drink," Slick said. "I fell off the damn mountain. Ain't none of us in any too good shape just now, so don't feel so damn special."

"I'm all over scratches and scrapes and bruises," Hedley said. "They done scabbed up, and whenever I bend a arm or a leg, they crack open again. Hurts like hell." He reached for his glass, and when he bent his elbow to raise it to his lips, he said, "Ow. Oh."

Cain pulled out a chair and sat down with a series of moans and groans. "Oh, hell," he said. "Ever'thing on me hurts. I ain't never walked that far in my whole life before. I don't never want to do it again neither. I want to kill those two bastards so bad, it makes my teeth hurt."

"We got to kill them," Slick said. "And we got to do it pretty damn quick."

"How the hell we going to do it?" Barber said. "We sure as hell didn't do so good last night. I hope someone of us has got a better plan than that one. We're lucky none of us got killed last night."

"I feel like I got killed," Hedley said.

"That's just stupid," said Barber. "If you'd a got killed, you wouldn't be feeling nothing."

"How do you know?" Hedley said. "You ever been killed? If you ain't never been killed, then you don't know if you feel something or not. All them dead folks out in the cemetery might be just suffering like hell for all you know."

"Bullshit," Barber said.

"We got to come up with something," said Cain. "They ain't done with us. We all know that. So Slick's idea for last night didn't work out so good. So we come up with another one. That's all. Has anyone looked out there this morning? Is them two still there at their little camp?"

"I ain't looked," Hedley said. "I'm afraid that if I was to look out that winder, one of them two bastards would shoot my fool head off."

"Hell," Barber said. "I'll look."

He took up the spyglass and walked along the wall until he reached the front of the room. Then he scooted along the front wall to the window. He peeked around the edge and looked toward the camp. He could see the fire burning, and he could see two figures sitting there. Unable to resist it, he put the spyglass to his eye and got a better look at each individual. Finally, he lowered the glass and slid around the walls again in order to go back to the table and join the others.

"Well?" Cain said.

"They're up there, all right," Barber said. "Just setting there like they ain't got a worry in the world. Smoking cee-gars and drinking coffee."

"Bastards," said Hedley.

"What are we going to do?" Barber asked.

"I hear riders coming up behind us," Foss said, standing up and taking his rifle with him. He moved to one edge of the makeshift tent to get a look. "Well, I'll be. Slocum, you need to get a look at this."

Slocum stood up and moved to Foss's side. He saw Millicent and Halley riding down the trail. He frowned. The women rode up closer, and Foss walked out to meet them. They dismounted.

"Thought maybe you run out of good grub," Halley said. "We brought some more."

"The good grub is more than welcome," Foss said, "but I wish you had stayed away."

"Well," Halley said, looking up at Slocum, "is that how you feel, too?"

"I couldn't have said it no better," he answered.

"That's a fine welcome," said Millicent with a lovely pout on her lips. Foss took her in his arms and pulled her close to him.

"I just don't want you getting in the way of any danger," he said.

"We know," Millicent said. "We met your barefoot cowboys."

"You have any problems with them?" Slocum asked.

"Nary a one," said Halley. "They was as nice as they could be. Hell, you all reformed them. They said when you come back for them, they was meaning to take them stolen horses back where they got them."

"I'm glad to hear that," said Foss.

"Well," Slocum said, "as long as you're here, let's go sit down and have some coffee and some good grub. I'll take care of your horses."

Slocum unsaddled the two horses and put them with the rest, while the women and Foss prepared the meal. They sat together around the fire and ate and visited. No one talked yet of killing, but the women were obviously both pleased and relieved to have found the two men alive and unhurt. The tension of the situation was palpable, though. Not one of them could help but notice that Slocum was almost constantly watching the town below, especially the front of the Booze Palace. He remembered the rifle shot that had taken the life of Murf Richie. He did not want a similar shot coming at them with the ladies present.

Millicent was exercising all her self-control to keep from telling Foss about Halley's offer. She knew that he had to keep his mind on business now, and she did not want to distract him, but she was terribly anxious to let him in on the good news. Slocum, in spite of his concentration on the front of the saloon, could sense that Millicent wanted Foss alone. He reached for the coffeepot and poured himself another cup.

"Say," he said, glancing over at Foss, "why don't you two take yourselves a little stroll back there somewhere out of the line of fire. I can keep an eye on things here all right. I don't really expect any surprises this morning any-how. They're all busy nursing their wounds down there."

"If you need me," said Foss, "give a yell." He stood and then gave Millicent a hand up, and they walked away from the camp. Now the temptation was too great. They were alone. The horrible business that he and Slocum were on did not seem real to her. She took his hand in hers and squeezed it tight.

"Amos," she said, "Halley has made us a wonderful offer." She went on to detail what Halley had proposed to her, how they would be partners, and how they would build a separate house. When she was through, she waited for his response, but it did not come fast enough to suit her. "Well," she said, "what do you say?"

"I don't know, darlin'," he said. "It's a fine offer. She's got a real nice place out there, and I'd love to have a place like that for you and me. But I don't know that I have a right to go cutting into her business. She's worked hard to build up what she's got out there and—"

"I thought about all that," she said. "Halley told me that she needs help. She wants us to stay. This offer was not made out of pity, Amos. It was a business decision. Think how much more could be done out there if she had help. Why, she even told me that she's already getting more done with me there just doing housework. Think about it, Amos. Will you?"

"Sure, I'll think about it," he said. "It's a generous offer. Maybe we'll all three sit down and talk it over after this business is done."

Halley also decided that the time was right for serious talk. She had Slocum alone. She figured that he might have some influence over Foss. "I made Millie an offer," she said.

"What kind of offer?" Slocum asked.

She explained the whole thing to him, and then she sat back and waited for a reaction. Slocum pulled a cigar out of his pocket and lit it in the campfire. He leaned back again, still watching the saloon below.

"It would work," he said. "Be good for all of you. Hell,

you'd likely get rich that way. You got a fine place, Halley, but it's too much for just you alone. The three of you could really make a go of it."

"Will you tell that to Amos?" Halley asked. "You know how a man is. He'll think I'm offering a handout. His pride will get in his way. Hell, Slocum, I ain't offering no handout, and I told that to Millie, but I'm afraid Amos'll take it that way. Will you bend his ear a little?"

"I will if I get a chance," Slocum said.

Halley sat back and relaxed, snuggling into Slocum's shoulder. "Hell," she said, "that's all I ask."

19

"Foss," Slocum said, "let's go down there and get this thing over with."

"All right," Foss said.

"I suggest we leave the rifles with the ladies," said Slocum. Then he turned to face Millicent and Halley. "I hope you don't need them, but if anyone comes this way, and you ain't sure of him, shoot him."

"You don't have to worry about that," Halley said.

"We going to ride down or walk?" Foss asked.

"It's a longer walk than I usually like to take," Slocum said, "but if leads starts flying, I don't want to have to deal with a horse. I'll walk it."

"I'll join you," Foss said.

Millicent suddenly threw her arms around Foss and held him tight. "Amos," she said, "do you have to do this?"

"I have to," he said.

"Then be careful," she said. "I want you to come back to me. I don't want you hurt."

"Try not to worry," he said. "I'll be careful. You can count on that. I'm looking real forward to coming back to you."

Halley threw an arm around Slocum's neck and kissed him on the mouth. "I know you ain't coming back to me," she said, "but I still want to see you come through this in one piece. Be careful."

"Well," Slocum said, "I don't know how this thing is going to turn out, but I sure as hell know how I mean for it to turn out, and I aim to work real hard to make it happen that way."

Slocum stepped away from Halley and turned to face Whizbang. He gave a hitch to his gunbelt, checked his Colt to make sure it was sliding easy out of the holster, then took a deep breath. Foss stepped up beside him. The two men gave each other a look. Then they started walking.

"Sammy," said Slick, "come here. Take a look."

Sammy Cain stood up with a groan and walked to the front window where Slick was standing and looking out.

"They're coming," he said. Barber and Hedley came running when they heard that. The four men crowded together at the broken window. They could see Slocum and Foss on foot, walking side by side, in the distance, moving down from the campsite.

"It's just the two of them," Hedley said.

"But looky," said Cain. "There's two more up at the camp. I knew there had to be some more to go along with all them horses."

"Sammy," Slick said, "you got your rifle with you?"

"Hell, no," said Cain. "You know I come limping back in here direct from up on top of that damned mountain. Besides, my shoulder's bruised. If I had it I couldn't use it."

"Damn," Slick said. "Anyone got a rifle gun?"

"You recollect what happened the last time Sammy took a rifle shot at them up there?" Hedley asked. "There's still at least two up at the camp. Likely they'd fill this place with bullets again, just like the last time."

"Who is that up at the camp?" Barber asked.

"I can't tell without that spyglass," said Slick. "Where is it?"

Barber and the others looked around. "Hell," said Barber, "I don't see it right now."

"If we don't pick them off," Slick said, "they'll be right down here with us in just a few minutes. Is that what you want?"

"What I want is clear out of this mess," said Hedley, "but that ain't going to happen."

"Not till you're dead," Barber said.

"All right. All right," said Slick. "How about this? Two of you slip across the street and get up on top of a building over there. Doc's place has a stairway in back. You can climb on up from the landing. Two of us will stay on this side and get up on top of the Palace here. When they come right into the middle of town, we'll blast them."

"We'd have to wait till they're almost down here," Cain said. "From where they are now, they can see ever' move we make."

"Besides that," said Hedley, "they still got rifles up there at the camp. If we was on the roof, they could sight in on us real easy."

"Damn it," Slick said. "You're right."

"I can't climb anyhow," said Cain. "I'm hurting all over too bad."

About a fourth of the way down the steep walk into town, Slocum noticed that people on the street had all gone inside somewhere. They must have noticed the approach of the two men and figured out what was about to happen. Except for some horses tied to hitch rails here and there, Whizbang looked like a ghost town.

"They know we're coming by now," he said to Foss. "They're bound to. Everyone else does."

"Yeah," said Foss.

"Keep your eyes peeled for any movement down there," Slocum said.

"If they move," said Foss, "I'll see them. My bet is they're in the saloon. Likely watching us through that busted-out front window. They might try to pick us off with rifle shots."

"If they do," Slocum said, "we'll see a rifle barrel poke out somewhere. Foss?"

"Yeah?"

"The first one you see, kill him. Don't try to be a lawman. Don't give him no warning. Just shoot, and shoot to kill."

"I will," said Foss.

Dutch came down the alley behind the Booze Palace. Like most everyone in town, he had seen Slocum and Foss coming, and he had figured that it was time for the showdown. He let himself in the back door, and almost immediately, he saw the four desperate wretches huddled at the front window. When they heard the door, they jumped. Slick pulled a revolver.

"It's Dutch," said Hedley.

"What are you boys up to?" Dutch asked.

"If you don't know," Slick said, "you're the only one in town."

"You know me, Gordie," said Dutch, moving toward the bar. "I never listen, so I never hear. I mind my own business. It's part of my job."

"Yeah, well, that Slocum and old Amos is coming down the hill," Hedley said. "They mean to kill us. That's what's going on."

"Yeah?" said Dutch. He was behind the bar by this time. "And what do you four mean to do? Hide in here and shoot them from ambush?"

Sammy Cain snorted. "You don't expect us to go out there in the street and face them professional killers, do you?"

"No, Sammy," said Dutch. "I guess you wouldn't do that. Even if there are four of you and only two of them. I guess you wouldn't do that at all. Not unless you were forced to."

He reached under the bar where a kerosene lamp was stashed, and he took out a match, struck it and lit the lamp. Then he moved the lamp up to the top of the bar. He turned the flame up high, and he checked the level of kerosene in the lamp. It was nearly full. The men at the window were not looking at him. They were all watching Slocum and Foss.

"They'll be down here in another minute," Hedley said. "What're we going to do?"

"You move over to the door," Slick said. "Three of us can shoot from right here. We'll just wait till they're right out there in front of us. With four guns blasting away at them, they'll go down. They'll be dead before they know what happened."

There was a sudden crash and whoosh, and the four surprised would-be bushwhackers jumped and looked behind them to see a wall of flame roaring and spreading fast across the middle of the room.

"Goddamn you, Dutch," Slick said. He jerked his revolver and fired a shot. Dutch clutched at his chest. He slumped over the bar and slid down to the floor. He was dead.

"We can't stay in here," said Hedley. "This whole place is going to go up."

"What'll we do?" Barber yelled.

"Stay calm," said Slick. "Maybe them two'll get on down here before the fire gets too close to us."

"They're moving pretty slow," said Cain. "The fire's spreading fast."

"It's damn hot already," said Hedley. "I ain't staying in here."

Hedley bolted for the door. Sammy Cain was right behind him. Barber gave Slick a nervous look. Slick looked toward the road.

"I don't see them," he shouted.

Barber looked toward the road, then back at the roaring flames, then again at Slick. He turned and ran out the front door into the street.

Up on the hillside road, Slocum and Foss had heard the shot. They shot each other quick glances, but they kept walking. A moment later they could see the flames through the front window of the Booze Palace.

"Now's our chance," said Slocum. "Let's go."

They ran the rest of the way down the hillside and into the town. By the time they were on the main street, flames were licking their way through the center of the rooftop of the Booze Palace. Slocum ran to the right side of the street, Foss to the left. They moved on toward the flames. Then they saw Hedley run from the burning building. He ran across the street, but he was met at the door of the doc's office by the doc holding a shotgun.

"Don't bring your fight in here," Doc said.

Frightened and confused, Hedley tried the next-door office, but found the door locked. He turned and ran back into the street. Just then, Cain came hobbling out to join him.

"We're trapped, Sammy," Hedley said. "No one'll let us in."

Barber came running out then and joined them.

"Where are those guys?" he asked.

The three men looked toward the road going up the hill and saw no one. Then Barber said, "Look. There's Amos."

All three men pulled their revolvers and started firing wildly. The distance was too great for accurate firing with revolvers. Amos Foss kept walking calmly. He held his own revolver at his side. Finally he stopped and raised his right arm. He took careful aim and fired. Hedley jerked and twitched. There was a hole just beneath his rib cage on his left side.

"Oh, my God," he said. "I'm hit."

Barber and Cain turned back toward the saloon, but the flames were roaring high. Down the street, Foss walked forward a few more steps. He aimed and fired again. This time his bullet smashed the right shoulder of Sammy Cain.

"Ahh!" Sammy shouted. "Damn you, Amos!" He shifted his revolver to his left hand and fired back, his shots all going wild. Barber turned to run toward the far end of town, just as Slocum tried a shot from his side of the street. Because his target moved away from him unexpectedly, the shot caught Barber in the right ass-cheek.

He screamed and fell forward, then started crawling toward the sidewalk.

Moving forward slowly and methodically, Foss and Slocum each fired again. Foss's shot hit the already severely wounded Hedley in the chest. Hedley pitched forward, dead. Slocum's last struck Sammy Cain in the forehead. The street was clear again except for the wriggling figure of Barber trying desperately to put some distance between himself and his pursuers. He looked back over his shoulder to see both men walking after him. He crawled over to the board sidewalk and turned to face them.

Knowing he could not get away, Barber raised his revolver and sighted at Foss. Slocum saw it. He wondered if Foss would be able to shoot down a wounded, groveling man. He didn't want to take a chance. He took quick aim and fired, hitting Barber in the center of the chest. Slowly, Barber lowered his gun hand. Slowly, he leaned forward until his chin rested on his chest. After that, he did not move.

Foss looked over at Slocum. He knew what Slocum had been thinking, and he knew that Slocum may have been right. He had been about to shout at Barber to lay down his weapon. But Barber had been one of Slocum's targets. Slocum had meant all along to kill the man. What if Foss had called out to Barber, and Barber had taken the ex-lawman's advice and put his gun down? Then Slocum would almost certainly have killed an unarmed man. He never meant for any of the original seven to surrender and be dealt with by the law.

Slocum stood there, not far from the flaming building behind him, and Foss thought that this man surely had come after the seven killers like a demon from hell. Suddenly there was an unearthly scream, and a figure leapt through the already shattered front window of the burning Booze Palace. Flames danced all over its back, from its shoulders, down both its legs. Foss's gun hand went up as he yelled at Slocum, "Look out!" He fired, and the figure jerked and spun, regained its balance, and ran out into the middle of the street, streaming flames behind itself. Foss fired again. The figure jerked again, screamed, fired two shots into the ground just in front of itself, and fell forward, a ball of flame.

Slocum looked at Foss. "Gordon Slick," said Foss. "It's all over."

Back up at the campsite, Slocum, Foss, Halley, and Millicent watched as the flames consumed the old saloon and made their way to the buildings next door on both sides. Citizens, looking almost like ants, raced wildly about with buckets of water, futilely fighting the merciless fire. Foss was holding Millicent tight with an arm around her shoulders.

"That's a sad sight," said Slocum.

"Yes," Millicent said. "A whole town going like that."

"I meant all that booze," Slocum said. "I could sure use a drink right now."

They all laughed at that, and when they stopped, Halley walked over to where her saddlebags lay on the ground. "I come prepared for just such an emergency," she said, and she pulled a bottle of brown liquid out of the bag. She handed it to Slocum.

"Well, I'll be damned," he said. "I knew you was a good woman the first time I set eyes on you."

He uncorked the bottle and handed it over to Foss. Foss took it and drank, then handed it back. Slocum offered it to Halley then, and she took a healthy gulp and offered the bottle to Millicent.

"Oh, no," Millicent said. "Thank you just the same. I—oh, hell, yes. Let me have a slug."

As Millicent took a drink, then coughed and held the bottle out away from herself, they all laughed again. Nothing was really as funny as it seemed to them at the time. The tremendous relief at having the violent business behind them had made them all a bit giddy. They knew that, too.

"Well," Halley said, "it's over. What'll you do now, Slocum?"

"I'll be moving on soon enough," Slocum said, "but I

was just thinking that you all are talking about building a house and all. You might could use a little help for a while. And I don't feel like hitting the trail again just yet, not after all this, well, you know—"

"Slocum," said Halley, "you hang around just as long as you like, and whenever you decide it's time to move on, won't nobody try to talk you out of it. Deal?"

"That's a deal, lady," Slocum said. He reached again for the bottle, and just then they saw a short, roundish man in a black suit coming toward them up the hill, struggling to make the climb. Slocum gave Foss a questioning look.

"That's Jim Baker," Foss said. "He's one of the surviving town council members."

"What does he want, I wonder," Halley said.

"He's an ugly little man," said Millicent. "I never did like him."

In another minute, Baker puffed his way into the camp. He took off his hat and wiped his forehead with his sleeve.

"Howdy," he said. "Well, you done it. You got them all. I never did quite understand just what all this was about, but I always figured that you'd be on the right side, Amos, whatever it was."

"You fired me, Baker," said Foss.

"Not me," Baker said. "Don't blame me personal for that. It was a vote of the town council, and we was all confused just then about what was going on around us. You can understand that, can't you?"

"Yeah," said Foss. "I guess I can." He glanced at Slocum. "I was a bit confused by it myself for a while there."

"Just what do you want here?" Slocum asked abruptly. Baker looked at Slocum, opened his mouth, then looked back at Foss.

"Amos," he said, "we just had an emergency meeting of the town council—what's left of it. And we all agreed. We want you to come back."

"Come back?" Foss said.

"We want you to take your old job back," said Baker. "Be our town marshal again. We need you, Amos. We'll build you a new jailhouse, better'n the old one. We'll even give you a pay raise. What do you say?"

Foss looked at Millicent. She looked back at him with an anxious eye. He glanced over at Halley. Then he said, "Naw, Baker, I don't think so. I got a better offer."

"We can sweeten the pot some," Baker said.

Foss pointed off generally toward the town. "I don't know what you're going to have left to sweeten it with," he said. "Looks to me like most of your town's going up in smoke."

"Hell," said Baker, "we can rebuild."

"I gave you my answer," Foss said, and Millicent snuggled up to his side. He put an arm around her. "Besides," he said, "a lawman has no business with a wife, and I'm fixing to get married to this lovely lady."

Baker looked astonished, almost unbelieving. He pointed at Millicent. "To tha—to that widow woman?" he said. "To that slut?" He snorted like a hog. "Goddamn, Amos, I'm fixing to save you from a fate worse than death. Hell, she was sneaking this here Slocum into her bed before she took you back there. Forget it, and take your old job back. We'll do you right."

Foss looked down at Millicent. She was blushing and ducked her head in shame. Foss gently pushed her to one side, then stepped up close to Baker. With no warning, he smashed Baker in the side of the head with a roundhouse right. Baker fell back and landed hard on his fat ass. Foss stepped in quickly, reached down to take Baker by his coat lapels, and jerked him to his feet. Then he turned him around, took hold of him by his collar and by the seat of his trousers and heaved him headlong down the hill.

"You reckon he understands that means no?" Slocum asked.

Foss turned to look at Slocum. Slocum started to speak, but Millicent interrupted him.

"Amos," she said, "I'm sorry I didn't—"

"Hush up," Foss said. "That Baker's always had a foul mouth. Don't any of you pay attention to one word he said. Hell, I've already forgot what he came up here about."

Halley decided to change the subject. "You told him you had a better offer," she said. "Does that mean we have a deal?"

Foss reached for Millicent again and pulled her to his side.

"It sure does, Halley," he said. "And we thank you for the offer. I can't make you any guarantees, but I'll sure work hard for our success."

"We'll work hard," said Millicent. "Together."

They rode up to the camp where the two barefoot cowboys waited anxiously. Bandy and Watson almost danced for joy when they saw them coming: the four riders, two men and two women, and all the extra horses. First thing when they rode into the camp, Slocum tossed the boys their boots. Amos Foss rode over close and held their gunbelts out to them. The cowboys just laid all those things aside, and they pumped the hands of their visitors vigorously.

"I'm sure glad to see you all back safe and sound," said Bandy.

"With your horses and guns," said Slocum.

"Well, that, too, Mr. Slocum," Bandy said, "but we're real glad to see you safe. Say, coffee's on. Y'all want some? We 'bout ate up all the food you left us."

"We've got more," Halley said. "Come on, Millie. Let's lay on a spread."

Everyone settled down around the fire while the women prepared the meal. The cowboys looked anxiously at Slocum and Foss.

"Mr. Slocum," said Bandy, "Mr. Foss, I don't know what the ladies here told y'all 'bout our visit, but while you was gone, me and Candy here done a lot of thinking, and we decided that you was right about us. Well, first off, you was right about them horses. We did steal them. And then we decided that you was right about them other things, too. We hadn't ought to be stealing things from folks. We ought to look harder for honest work."

"Well, we figured—"

Bandy hesitated and Walker jumped in to help him out.

"We figured that we'd take them horses back where we got them," he said. "If you'll let us. If you don't trust us, well, you could ride along with us to make sure we get it done. You were fair with us, and we want to do right. That's all."

Slocum and Foss looked at one another.

"These boys ride back where they stole those horses," Slocum said, "someone's liable to shoot them."

"Shoot them dead," said Foss.

"On the other hand," Slocum said, "maybe if we was to ride along with them, maybe one of us could ride ahead and sort of smooth things over for them."

"Maybe," Foss said.

"And it might go even better for them," Slocum said, "if they was able to say they had them a job at a little horse ranch somewhere."

The two cowboys' eyes opened wide and they leaned forward to listen to all this.

" 'Specially," said Halley, butting into the conversation, "if that little ranch was part run by a well-known ex-lawman, name of Amos Foss."